WILD AND WILLING

Joanne Rock

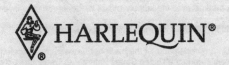

HARLEQUIN®

TORONTO • NEW YORK • LONDON
AMSTERDAM • PARIS • SYDNEY • HAMBURG
STOCKHOLM • ATHENS • TOKYO • MILAN • MADRID
PRAGUE • WARSAW • BUDAPEST • AUCKLAND

To Linda Watson, the sister I have forever looked up to for great advice, a grounded perspective and much-needed laughter. Thank you for providing a Florida consultation hotline as I penned this book!

And to Wanda Ottewell, my talented editor, whose vision and guidance have strengthened my writing and made my work all the more rewarding.

RECYCLED PAPER · RECYCLED PAPER

ISBN 0-373-79058-9

WILD AND WILLING

Copyright © 2002 by Joanne Rock.

This edition published by arrangement with Harlequin Books S.A.

® and TM are trademarks of the publisher. Trademarks indicated with ® are registered in the United States Patent and Trademark Office, the Canadian Trade Marks Office and in other countries.

Visit us at www.eHarlequin.com

Printed in U.S.A.

1

SETH CHANDLER flipped up his eye patch and leaned against the ship mast of the *Jose Gaspar* to study the throng of milling pirates aboard the main deck. He could think of a thousand places he would rather yo-ho-ho with a bottle of rum today.

His empty office full of paperwork topped the list.

There had to be seventy-five guys and a couple of women in swashbuckling gear sailing into Tampa Bay with him, yet Seth hadn't been able to pawn off today's mission on any of them. Not with *his* company's name on the line as corporate sponsor of this event.

Damn that lead buccaneer for quitting only two hours before Tampa's annual Gasparilla festival. Now Seth had no choice but to step in and assume the eye patch himself. He'd spent too many years building his company's reputation to have it compromised by any screwups with this very public assignment.

Someone had to abduct a wench.

Actually, several festivalgoers would be carried off by the marauding raiders, but the lead pirate at the front of the boat would no doubt be captured on film for the six o'clock news. When the actor hired to play the role had quit, Seth hadn't wanted to hand over the part to just anyone. What if his last-minute fill-in copped a feel in full view of the media? Or what if the stand-in dropped the person he was supposed to be carrying?

Lawsuit alert!

Without résumés and references in front of him, Seth wouldn't risk it. He'd strapped on a dagger, stripped out of his shirt, kicked off his Italian loafers and vaulted barefoot aboard the *Jose Gaspar* at the last minute.

Now, as the ship sailed at the head of a flotilla around Harbour Island toward thousands of waiting festival attendees on shore, Seth wished he hadn't been born so damn responsible. He didn't want to spend his Saturday leering at giggling maidens as part of the festival's entertainment.

Seth scanned the crowds lining the docking area in front of the convention center, searching for appropriate candidates for mock abduction. He dismissed the hordes of tourists braving the mild February weather in string bikinis. The last thing he needed was some racy media photo of himself with a beach babe thrown over his shoulder. He was definitely going for a local—a woman with enough clothes on to ensure he wouldn't look like a sleazeball for touching too much bare skin.

Bad enough *he* was half-naked. He didn't need the added trouble—or temptation—of a scantily clad woman in his arms.

All he had to do was find a safe woman, maybe a grandmotherly type, who would enjoy the adventure and generate great P.R. for Chandler Enterprises. He'd carry her off to the boat his brother had waiting for him, then treat her to dinner for her trouble. He could bring her back to the city later tonight.

Simple.

Piece of cake, in fact, for a man who managed international mergers, could read financial newspapers in a dozen languages and had compiled enough venture capital to support himself and a small army for the rest of their lives.

He slapped his eye patch back down over his brow and clamped his teeth around a blunt dagger as the ship moved into position in front of the partiers on shore.

How much trouble could abducting a wench possibly be?

MIA QUENTIN elbowed her way to the front of the string bikini crowd, hoping to catch a peek at the incoming ship full of pirates, her last chance for adventure. Determined to put herself in the path of the first marauding invader she spied, Mia simmered with restless energy and uncharacteristic daring.

Damned if she didn't feel downright dangerous.

She tucked a red hibiscus behind her ear and draped long brown hair over her shoulder. She just hoped one of those pirates appreciated a more artistic approach to fashion than a bikini made of dental floss. Mia happened to think her long floral sarong and black silk halter-top were much more evocative than the blatant message sent by miles of naked legs.

Then again, her knowledge of seduction was about as limited as the other women's scanty outfits. She'd been avoiding adventure—and men—for the past three years. Somehow she'd ended up practically celibate in an effort to assure her grandparents she wasn't following in the footsteps of her reckless mother—a woman who'd missed most of Mia's childhood in favor of chasing any surfer skimming past her beach lounger.

But Mia wasn't in her Twin Palms hometown now. She'd carved out a whole week to play in Tampa before she had to get down to business—wheedling a few months' extension from the bank on a mortgage note for the family tourist shop.

For now, Mia had promised herself she would stop living for her family and start living more for herself.

She'd realized in recent months that she'd slowly retreated from the world because she didn't ever want to upset the grandparents she adored. This notion slammed home with a vengeance last week when a vendor had brought some sample wares to the tourist shop. As Mia inverted a cheesy, water-filled pen that made a cartoon guy's pants fall down, it occurred to her that that was as close as she'd come to a titillating experience in too many years.

So this week, she planned to prove to herself she still knew how to have fun, to be adventurous. Once she secured the mortgage extension on the tourist shop, she'd be working double time to make sure the business could really pay it off. So if ever there'd been a time to have fun, the time was *now,* before she disappeared into a world of work and family obligations again.

And if an opportunity arose this week to see a real man naked, she certainly wouldn't be averse to peeking.

Mia lifted a small pair of opera glasses to her eyes in order to better drool over the wealth of muscle-bound men aboard the incoming ship. But before she could focus on the testosterone-laden *Jose Gaspar,* a scratchy voice beside her interrupted.

"You don't stand a chance in that getup, honey." The speaker was a woman at least seventy years old with white hair cut short in a sleek, sophisticated style. She wore a long green beach robe belted at her waist, which she slowly unfastened. "You've got to show a little leg."

On cue, the older woman's terry cloth cover-up fell open, revealing legs that would give Mia's a run for the money. Mia hoped she looked that good in fifty years. On the other hand, she hoped she could hold her own against grandma today.

Because Mia had her heart set on a sexy abduction scenario with a pirate.

"You're sure to turn a few heads," Mia admitted. "But I don't think my outfit lends itself to—"

The older woman squinted down at Mia's wrap skirt. "Let me see." She bent closer, ignoring any polite sense of personal boundaries to adjust the knot at Mia's waist. "All you need to do is twist this here and turn this—" She tugged and pulled until, "Voila!"

Mia stared down at the new slit in her sarong and the long expanse of tanned leg it showcased.

The older woman winked, her open robe twirling loosely around her legs as she moved. "If you've got it, flaunt it, honey."

Mia wasn't convinced what she had was entirely flauntable, but she had to admit, the woman's fashion sense had flair. The sarong had a sexy edge with the newly arranged slit. Now the warm February breeze tickled her skin as it blew the gauzy fabric around her thighs.

And it was still more mysterious than a dental floss swimsuit.

"Thanks." Mia smiled up at the woman, but the granny fairy godmother was already edging her way closer to the docking area where the boat would anchor.

Not to be outdone, Mia hustled into the slight opening in the crowd in the woman's wake. It was every maiden for herself when it came to nabbing a pirate.

She needed this adventure today. She'd been suppressing her own dreams the past few years while she peddled seashell necklaces and driftwood picture frames. This might be her last chance for a little excitement before she returned to the watchful eyes of her small-town beachside home.

She'd spent her life always doing the right thing, but not today. In order to get what she wanted, Mia was prepared to be bold and brazen.

And she wasn't going to let any kindly grandmothers or overzealous beach bunnies stand in her way.

"SEE ANYTHING you like, matey?"

The pirate standing next to Seth gestured to the massive mob of women on the shore, his question thick with a swashbuckling accent. Patrick O'Keefe led the Gasparilla Krewe on the boat. A retired Tampa business professional, Pat could afford to put all his time into the festival.

Seth tried to work up the enthusiasm for a hearty "Aye" in return, but only managed a rather flat, "Yeah. I've already got the right woman picked out."

Pat slapped him on the back and off he went to quiz the handful of other people who were on abduction missions today.

A cry went up from the festivalgoers as the boat bumped into the docking area in front of Tampa's convention center. Television cameras moved in closer to film the new arrivals, shuffling the crowd as they dragged their equipment around for a better view.

Seth kept his eye trained on his wench of choice—a woman old enough to be his grandmother in an old-fashioned green swimsuit and matching long beach robe.

It was simple enough to keep track of the white-haired lady. Not only did her bright green robe set her apart from the hordes of half-dressed sunseekers, but she was being relentlessly pursued by a lithe brunette dressed in a silky skirt with an oversize red flower tucked behind her ear.

A gorgeous, lithe brunette.

With great legs.

Seth squinted against the glare of a too-bright sun

to get a better look. Not that he had any intention of carrying off an exotic, showy woman who could have just stepped out of a local theater production of *Carmen*. She was too conspicuous, too racy, too sexy.

But damn, she was hot.

Long brown hair fell to the middle of her back— a bare back that he could half see from his raised position on the boat. Her features suggested Italian-American heritage. Maybe Hispanic-American. Something Latin looking.

Her skirt was sort of filmy and Seth guessed he'd be able to see through it if she stood in front of a bright light. Every now and then as she darted through the mob of festivalgoers, Seth caught a view of lean, tanned thigh between the folds of gauzy material.

"Land ho, me boy," Patrick O'Keefe shouted, gesturing toward the docking area. "I need you to lead the charge off the boat."

Show time. Seth searched for some enthusiasm for his task, half considering revamping the abduction strategy so he could make off with Carmen instead of her grandmother. He definitely wouldn't mind an up close and personal perusal of those legs of hers.

And it had been at least…four months?…since his most recent relationship flopped. Margo had marched out the door citing the usual laundry list of his short-comings—obsessive commitment to his work, single-minded pursuit of success, inability to form a true partnership, etc. No wonder a set of great legs distracted him today.

He closed his eyes in an effort to scavenge some last-minute focus. The only thing that mattered right now was that the Gasparilla event ran smoothly so it would reflect well on its sponsor, Gulf Coast Bank, one of many branches of Chandler Enterprises. Seth would wait until later to worry about the fact that he'd been without female companionship for too long.

Right now, he was grabbing grandma for good P.R. value and making a clean getaway in his waiting boat.

Patrick threw a rope to the men on shore so the *Jose Gaspar* could be tied off. "Don't forget to return yer lady of choice to the reviewing stand by 11:00 p.m. tonight," he reminded Seth. "The local networks are giving us a slot on the late news, and we want all the pirate captives available to talk about their day."

Eleven? That was still six hours away, even with the festival getting off to a late start this year due to a thunderstorm.

"Don't worry," Seth shot back, trying—and failing—to keep his eyes from straying to Carmen. "I'll have her here in plenty of time."

Patrick frowned. "The point is to show the lady a good time." The old man waggled bushy eyebrows. "If you bring her back *too* early, we'll think you didn't do your pirately duty by her."

Seth nodded, unconcerned. He had a vested interest in making sure his captive waxed enthusiastic about her day for the cameras. "I'll keep that in mind."

A buzz of excitement passed through the festival attendees as the final knots were tied to secure the *Jose Gaspar*. Seth shifted his position onboard to put him closest to his maiden of choice. And the siren alongside her.

He didn't wait for the lowering of the gangplank. Pirates seldom did, right?

Fully committed to the role he'd taken on, Seth vaulted off the low boat and into the waiting crowd a few feet below. The excited buzz swelled into a roar of approval from the bustling throng. Other pirates swung out over the crowd, the invasion well underway.

He landed farther from his target than he'd intended, but that didn't stop him from going after the woman he wanted. A Nordic-looking blonde planted herself in his path, and shot him a sleepy-lidded invitation steamy enough to sizzle the shorts off a man.

She was impressive, but she didn't come close to Carmen. Seth set her aside with a wink and a nod, determined to run away with the green-robed granny and a big headline in tomorrow's papers.

Too bad he sorely underestimated Carmen's appeal. No sooner had he turned away the blonde than *she* was there. The brunette who had been shadowing granny—the one who'd caught his eye before his sea legs even hit dry land.

The crowd surged behind him, pushing him toward her even though his whole body had stopped dead a foot away from her. All at once, she was plastered against him, a slender but curvy-in-all-the-right-places body molded to his for one sensory over-loading second before she stepped back an inch.

Heat simmered through his veins, nerve endings he hadn't been aware of leapt to life, greedy for an-other round with the devastatingly feminine physique of the woman standing in front of him.

Who was *not* the woman he was supposed to grab, some annoyingly logical part of his brain insisted on reminding him.

Damn.

His mouth was so dry he didn't stand a chance of eking out a "pardon me." Not when her green cat eyes probed over him with slow thoroughness. Bad enough she licked her lips as her gaze wandered over his bare chest. But then she took her perusal a bit lower, and her full, pink lips curved into a smile.

God was not playing fair today. This was surely more temptation than one well-meaning man could possibly endure, wasn't it?

Seth could carry her off on his boat for a few hours and lose all his cares in the warmth of her blatant invitation. He reached for her, effectively shutting off the practical side of his brain for two seconds.

Until the rolling base of a television camera ran over his foot at the same time a microphone appeared in between them.

Shit.

Cold reason returned, barely nudging out the heat pulsing through him. But he was on a mission, damn it, and he'd always prided himself on putting his company first. Every member of his family had money tied up in Chandler Enterprises and Gulf

Coast Bank because they trusted Seth to think with his brain and not his...well, they trusted him.

Swallowing his regrets, Seth spun on his heel and reached for the green terry cloth beside Carmen. He would abduct granny because he was here on business. His wayward attraction to the bold brunette would only get him into trouble today.

Seth braced his feet to hoist the white-haired older woman into his arms, but instead of reeling in green terry cloth, Seth found himself with a red hibiscus tickling his nose.

Carmen had somehow twirled her way into his arms and glued herself to his chest.

Cold reason made a feeble attempt at resistance. His logical brain assured him this was not going according to his well-laid plans.

But before he could do anything about it the television cameras zoomed in on Carmen.

Right about the moment she started screaming.

2

MIA PREPARED TO belt out another round of mock terror for the big camera marked Channel 10, but the pirate stud beside her finally took the hint.

She'd been worried that, despite her best efforts, the bare-chested buccaneer would choose someone else to play "ravish the maiden" with. But engaging the media cameras and screaming her lungs out seemed to convince him she would be more fun than the hot-to-trot grandma in green.

Her brown-eyed Captain Kidd scooped her off her feet and into his arms, cradling her high against his chest.

Mia's artfully tied sarong fell away from her legs to drape over his arm, exposing her thigh to unadulterated contact with one steely bicep.

Mmm.

Playing to the camera—or maybe just playing for the pleasure of it—Mia threw her arms about the pirate's neck. Her silk-covered breasts grazed against his bare chest, the closest contact she'd had with any man for much, much too long. Heat prickled over her skin, anticipation curled low in her belly. Her adventure had officially begun.

And it felt wickedly delicious.

She winked and waved at the camera before she realized what she was doing. No doubt, someone in Twin Palms would be watching the five o'clock news on Channel 10. And with the way gossip traveled in a small town, her grandparents would think she was on her way to a life of dissolution by 5:05.

She turned her head into the crook of her captor's neck and whispered into the warmth of his soap-scented skin. "Let's get out of here."

He flexed his fingers, squeezing his hold on her just a little tighter. "You stage your own abduction and now you're in charge of the getaway, too?"

His smooth baritone held a note of amused censure, but he put his feet in motion before all the words left his mouth.

Deftly, he turned their bodies sideways for better aerodynamics to slice through the crowd of onlookers.

"I'd rather not be on the evening news," she informed him, surprised that her weight didn't seem to slow him down a bit. He navigated a path to the water's edge as easily as if he walked alone.

She tried not to notice the interesting ripple of his abs as he moved. The play of muscle along her hip sorely distracted her.

"Could have fooled me. That performance of yours looked tailor-made for TV." He glanced over his shoulder in the direction of the cameras they'd left behind.

"No. That performance was tailor-made for you." She'd promised herself she'd be bold today, and she wouldn't back down from her goal, even if the half-naked man she'd set her sights on was a bit more intimidating than the sailor in a striped shirt she'd originally envisioned for this scenario.

She forced herself to recall he wasn't really a pirate. No eighteenth-century man would have access to aftershave that smelled as sexy as this man's.

"All that screaming and jumping into my arms was for *my* benefit?" He slowed his stride as they neared a docking area about a hundred yards north of the convention center. "Does that mean you know me, Carmen? Because I sure as hell would remember if I knew you."

"Carmen?" Had she missed something? Maybe all those masculine pheromones were distorting her ability to remember her own name.

"You know, the aria-singing gypsy girl." He nodded toward the hibiscus behind her ear. "I guess it's the dark hair and the red flower."

"Oh." The analogy sounded wildly exciting. No one in Twin Palms would ever think of comparing her to an opera heroine. To them, she was just the Quentins' granddaughter. "I'm Mia Quentin. And no, we've never met."

Captain Kidd took a few more steps down a pier, his bare feet silent on the wooden planks. "I'm Seth Chandler. Care to tell me why you made it your mission to shriek your way in between me and the woman I planned to steal off with today?"

She hadn't intended to be quite *that* bold this afternoon. But once she'd gotten a good view of Seth, she'd grown even more committed to her plan.

"Were you really going for a woman twice your

age?'' Did that sound too rude? ''I mean, she had great legs and all, but—''

Seth set her on her feet with a thud at the end of the pier. ''Don't sweat it. Turns out Granny had her eye on another pirate anyway. Just before we left I saw her lock lips with our Krewe leader.''

''Good.'' The knowledge soothed her somewhat as she stared down at a sleek white cabin cruiser tethered to the dock. ''I'd hate to think I spoiled a rendezvous for you two.''

''You didn't.'' He stepped off the pier and into the sleek boat. ''But that doesn't answer my question.'' He held out his hand to draw her aboard. ''Why me?''

His question barely registered in her brain. Some last vestige of her reasonable self chose that moment to rear its head and ask her what the hell she was thinking to hop into a speedboat with a knife-wielding pirate she didn't know from Adam.

Seth released a frustrated sigh and gestured to the dock behind her. ''Unless you want to be tonight's feature story, I suggest you hightail it into the boat.''

Mia chanced a glance over her shoulder and discovered a small fleet of journalists headed their way. Members of the media jogged down the sidewalk toward the wooden pier, dragging cameras and microphones along with them.

The sight made Mia's decision for her. She leaped in the boat with both feet. ''A cruise on the Bay sounds very inviting.''

Seth popped switches at the helm and fired the engine. ''A *pleasure* cruise.'' He flashed her a grin that was pure pirate. His half-naked body brushed against hers as he crossed the deck to untie the boat. "I can't think of a better way to spend the day."

Mia urged him to hurry, even as she wondered what she was getting herself into. She had a can of mace in her purse, however, and a crowd of people had seen them leave together. The guy would *have* to know he didn't stand a chance of getting away with anything. Besides, she'd long-ago developed the ability to size up a man given the astonishing number of males her mother brought around. And Mia sensed a reassuring nobility in her bare-chested brigand.

Seth untethered them and slid back into his seat on the bridge, efficiently maneuvering out of the docking area with one hand, and peeling off his eye patch with the other.

Mia peered back toward land as they pulled away, but only until she noticed the lens of the television camera trained on them. Trying not to panic, she flung herself onto the bench seat just behind the steering wheel.

And right next to Seth. The man who'd said he was ready for a pleasure cruise.

Now things were starting to get interesting.

Mia straightened the flower in her hair, hoping she hadn't forgotten how to flirt. She'd done so successfully in college—before her family had nearly run the tourist shop into the ground and her mother had single-handedly given Grandpa an ulcer.

Once Mia returned to Twin Palms from her art program at the University of Miami, she'd forgotten all about dating. Too many responsibilities to worry about as she'd bailed Grandma and Grandpa out of near bankruptcy. Then, after she'd stabilized their finances—barely—and was ready to start seeing people again, she quickly realized her grandparents worried themselves sick any time she went out with anyone but the boy next door.

And as upstanding and polite as Frankie the marina manager might be, Mia had no interest in him.

Thus went her social life. Until now.

"You really think it's going to be a pleasure cruise?" Mia prompted, not caring if her fishing for reassurance was blatantly obvious. "Can I take that to mean you've sort of resigned yourself to me?"

Seth kicked the engines into a higher gear as they moved away from the flotilla and out of the main channels of traffic. Everyone in Tampa wanted to be at the festival but them.

"Depends." He risked a glimpse at her now that the waterway had cleared out. "Are you ever going to answer my question?"

Had he asked her a question? Mia found it difficult to remember as he pinned her with dark eyes. Without the eye patch, she got the full impact of his intent gaze.

Her temperature climbed a few notches.

"What question?"

He shook his head and checked the channel, easing the boat around a barrier island toward open water. "What gives with the theatrics today? Why make a big deal out of planting yourself in my path if we don't even know one another?"

"Oh, *that* question." Mia created and discarded

several answers before settling on the truth. "I'm looking for adventure. I thought being carried off by a pirate fit the bill quite nicely."

She waited, worried. Would he kick her off the boat now that she'd admitted to scheming? Launch into an offended diatribe about roping him into her plot?

As they left the last of marine congestion behind them, Seth turned up the engines and the boat roared to full speed. Determined not to let her adventure end yet as the wind and water sprayed her face, Mia thought she could at least make a stab at enticing him, let him see her ideas for fun and excitement might be worth pursuing after all.

The scent of the bay, a pungent blend of fish and boat fuel, drifted through the air. The rumble of the engine and splash of water drowned out any sounds around them, insulating their world with white noise.

"I'm not really Blackbeard, you know," Seth warned her, steering the cruiser into an occasional wave so that the spray kicked back all the more. "You're not going to find much adventure with me."

Says you.

Mia rose up on her feet, bracing herself on the broad band of windshield around the helm. She tipped her face into the spray and let the latest white-cap douse her.

Cool water sluiced over her, awakening her senses even though it barely diminished the warmth she experienced any time she so much as glanced at Seth.

All sense of caution washed away, Mia wrung out the water in her skirt as she stared down at him.

"Whoever you are, Seth Chandler, you're all the excitement a girl could want on a pleasure cruise."

WATER, WATER everywhere and not a frigging drop to drink.

Seth's mouth had never been so parched as he tracked rivulets of H_2O streaming down Mia Quentin's exposed thigh. She tugged at the soggy floral fabric tied around her hips, revealing more and more tanned leg as she twisted the hem to squeeze out excess water.

He struggled to think, to edge words past his dry lips. "You really don't know who I am."

She shrugged, a provocative move on a woman bending forward. Seth caught a glimpse of red lace in the vee of her black silk blouse.

"Seth Chandler the pirate who says he's not really a pirate. What more is there to know?" She straightened, allowing the damp, filmy skirt to fall back against her thighs.

Seth dragged his eyes up from a slow cataloguing of the way the fabric molded to her legs. Somewhere in the background of his lust-drenched thoughts, his brain screamed at him to pay attention to what she was saying.

"I guess there isn't much more to know."

"You work for Gulf Coast Bank?" She moved to the seat beside him, casually taking in the controls on the bridge.

He tensed. Did he work for the bank? Hell, Chandler Enterprises owned the bank, among other things. Maybe she knew who he was better than she let on.

She gestured to his pirate garb when he said nothing. "I mean, they were the corporate sponsors of Gasparilla, so I assume you work for them?"

Seth gauged her expression calling upon the ability to read people that had always served him well in business. He saw nothing but openness and honesty in Mia's face. Relaxing, he assured himself she had no clue about his real identity—an intriguing aspect of Mia Quentin. Every woman Seth had dated in the past knew his net worth to the penny. A circumstance that could occasionally make a guy wonder if he was being dated for himself or his checkbook.

But Mia had wanted *him*. Sure, she'd picked him out because of an eye patch. But she was still here now, flashing glimpses of killer thigh, driving him to the edge of sanity along with the constant niggling reminder that he hadn't had sex in four months.

The responsible thing to do would be to fess up. Too bad Seth had exceeded his quota of responsible acts for the week. He was more interested in seeing what would happen with Mia today.

"I do some work for the bank and a few other places. I'm sort of a go-to guy when they don't have anybody else to take care of special projects." Which was true.

"A Florida version of the Hollywood gopher?"

"Sort of." Which was not true. At all. He didn't want to explain who he was or what he did just yet, but he didn't want to totally misrepresent himself, either.

He pointed the boat south and shuffled the conversation in another direction before he dug himself any deeper. "What do *you* do when you're not out accosting unsuspecting men?"

"I'm in transition." Her hibiscus drooped in her damp hair so she plucked it out and cradled the red bloom between her palms. "I'm helping my grandparents fortify their family business right now, but when I'm not balancing books and doing inventory, I like to think of myself as an artist."

His view of her shifted to accommodate this new information. He watched her smooth her fingers over the petals of the flower, as if savoring the fragile texture.

"What kind of artist?" He leaned back in his seat, the boat requiring less of his attention now that they skimmed open water.

"Mostly I paint. I sculpt a little for fun, but I have more talent for painting—oils, watercolors, you name it." She glanced up from her flower to meet his gaze. "Where are we headed anyway?"

Something about the way she changed the subject made Seth suspect she didn't want to talk about herself. Or maybe her art.

"I thought we'd hit Egmont Key." Too intrigued by the vision of Mia with a paintbrush to let the subject drop, Seth continued to probe. "What subjects do you like to paint? People? Landscapes?"

"I paint anything. But I'm not much of a realist. My work tends to be more colorful, more vivid than the real world."

"That doesn't surprise me." He let his gaze roam over Mia's floral skirt, her oversize flower. "You're like a walking hothouse. In fact, this is the most damn colorful day I've had in a long time.''

''That probably has more to do with the cutlass and the eye patch.'' She crossed her legs, one toe pointing toward him, her foot mere inches from his calf.

He would definitely be jumping the gun if he reached over and pulled her against him. But he wanted to. Thinking about how much he wanted to delayed his response by several bracing, deep breaths.

''No, it's you. I normally live in black and white, and trust me, I know a Technicolor kind of woman when I see one.''

''Then my adventure must be a success so far.'' Her smile lit up her whole face, animating her eyes, drawing attention to her sensual mouth. ''How far is Egmont Key?''

Ten minutes was too far. Seth wanted nothing more than to stop the boat and talk to Mia. Stare at Mia. Find out if there was any chance he could have a relationship with a woman so different from any he'd ever known.

''Not much further. We'll have time to wander around the island and still make it back for the press conference at eleven tonight.''

''Press conference?'' She stiffened. The hibiscus stilled between her palms.

''Channel 10 is going to do a follow-up story on the people who were carried off by the Gasparilla pirates today. You'll have a chance to tell your story tonight on the news.''

Was it his imagination, or did she look panicked?

He slid one hand over her dark brown hair, surprised how silky the strands felt even after being tossed about by the wind. "Don't worry, we'll keep things PG-rated for the viewers at home."

She shook her head. "I can't go on television."

"It's good public relations for the bank—"

"But not good public relations for me!"

How could Carmen, who could bring a pirate to his knees, be afraid of a little media exposure? "Why?"

She folded her arms over her body, her lips firmly sealed.

Her refusal to discuss the topic couldn't have been any more eloquent.

"If you're married, lady, you're going to be riding the first wave back to shore." Seth clutched the steering wheel, ready to take her home.

Until he saw the surprise scrawled across her face.

"No!" Mia shook her head. "Married? I don't have room in my life for dating, let alone a husband. I assure you, I'm not married."

Again, the honesty in her eyes convinced him. He believed her.

But damn it, Seth needed that publicity tonight. He'd bought the sponsorship for Gulf Coast Bank because he desperately needed some public recognition. A growing financial institution with small-town roots, it was the kind of business Seth loved to build. But after floundering in a sluggish economy for the past year, Gulf Coast needed the visibility boost Gasparilla could offer.

And, bottom line, the bank needed the extra airtime he and Mia could garner with their story.

"I've got it." He snapped his fingers, pleased with himself. "If you go on the air and talk about our day together, you can also plug your paintings. You must have some for sale somewhere, right? You can talk about your next gallery showing or whatever."

Interest flashed in her eyes for all of two seconds before her chin tilted her up and she shook her head. "Sorry, Seth. I can't."

"Why?" Was he so wrong to ask for an explanation? It's not like he wanted to know so he could talk her into it in spite of her wishes. He wanted to know so that he could understand her, figure her out.

For a Technicolor artist, she was sure doing her best to keep part of herself hidden, shadowed.

Her fingers went back to their slow inventory of the hibiscus blossom, easing over each red petal.

"I make it a policy not to kiss and tell."

He recognized that answer for what it was. A seductive rerouting of his thoughts to get him off her case.

Damned if it didn't work like a charm.

His gaze flashed from red flower petals to soft red lips. It didn't take him but two seconds to make the decision to cut the boat engines and concentrate on her.

"Planning on kissing your abductor?" His question hovered in the air. Without the hum of the motor, the only sound around them came in the form of water lapping the sides of the boat.

And their breathing.

Hers soft and even. His shallow and quick.

"I thought we already established that I'm the one in charge of this so-called abduction today." With slow precision, Mia reached forward to set her flower on the helm, leaving her hands free, empty.

Seth picked up those hands and placed them on his shoulders, urged them around his neck.

"You thought wrong." He slid his hands around her waist. The silk of her blouse was already dry, warmed by her skin beneath it. "Kissing is my domain, Carmen, and I'm going to kiss you for two reasons."

She shifted closer, bringing with her the vague fragrance of exotic flowers, hothouse scents like jasmine or maybe orchids.

"I think reasoning defeats the point of kissing," she whispered, her husky tone a siren's song.

Determined to convince himself there was a reason for this kiss, Seth forged ahead, hovering closer to her lips. "First, kissing should be a part of any adventure."

"Oh, I'm with you there." Her green eyes locked on his, enticing him with sensual promise, urging him to forget his dumb-ass logic.

Without conscious permission, his fingers fanned out from his palms, reaching for new terrain over Mia's gentle curves.

He swallowed. Hard. "And second," he had to clear his throat as she wriggled beneath his hands, her body closing in on his. "I hear kissing can loosen the lips of women who won't reveal their secrets."

Mia tilted her head to one side, her gaze dipping

down to his lips and then back up to his eyes. A slow
smile curled her lips.

"Then by all means, sailor, give it your best
shot."

3

FROM THE MOMENT Seth's lips touched hers, Mia realized this was a man who knew how to mix business with pleasure.

Pleasure abounded in his kiss, washing over her in waves as surely as if she dived into the undulating waters of the Gulf. His tongue tangled with hers, calling her to take a few risks in her life, to come and play for a change.

Yet the kiss held the down-to-business quality of a man on a mission, too. This was no casual exploration of mutual interest. The steady pressure of Seth's body against hers told Mia in no uncertain terms that he wanted more, much more, than this kiss would give them.

Her heart rate sped, stamped out a heavy beat against her chest. His hands shifted up her body, brushing the sides of her breasts. Desire shot through her in automatic, irrefutable answer. Her silk top posed little barrier to the sensation of his warm fingers teasing her skin.

Kissing wasn't at all like she remembered it in her college days. Oh, she'd shared a brief peck with Frankie the marina guy in Twin Palms, but she hadn't *really* locked lips with anyone since her days at the University of Miami.

And although she'd had her share of fun back then, those college boys obviously hadn't known what the hell they were doing. Their kisses hadn't been so thorough, so deep, so...sexual.

The salty air, the sultry breeze over her skin, the briny scents of the sea, it all seemed so sexual. Sensation coiled between her thighs, a vivid pulse of pleasure that had never surfaced from just a kiss before.

"Oh my." She whipped her hand up between them, bracing it between Seth's chest and her own while bracing *her* against a tide of unexpected sensation in her most secret places.

"That's just what I was thinking," he whispered over her lips before indulging in another heady, roll-right-through-her kiss.

His tongue tangled with hers in obvious mating. He suckled her lower lip, drawing on the soft flesh in a way that sent her imagination spinning into overdrive.

His leg brushed against hers, his chest grazed her breast despite the barrier of her hand. The heady friction of their bodies created a seductive swirl of heat. Never had kissing seemed like such a microcosm of the sex act, so rife with innuendo of heady pleasures waiting for them....

The warmth inside her built, mounted, threatened to bowl her over. She couldn't be feeling what she thought she was feeling. Not now. Not from just a kiss.

But then waves rocked the boat, swayed her whole body in a provocative rhythm that mirrored the seductive thrust and recede of actual intercourse until...

"Oh!" She couldn't help the squeal of surprise, astonishment and all-out delight as an orgasm squeezed her insides, penetrated her every nerve ending. Sensation rocked her, saturating her senses and raining pleasure over every last cell of her body.

Oh my.

If Seth harbored any shock over her suddenly falling apart in his arms, he didn't let on. Instead, he merely groaned in time with her rapturous sigh, echoing her pleasure as if it were his own.

He kissed her another moment before sliding away from her, leaving her wilted and only semisated— and still in total shock—on the helm seat.

Silence reigned in the aftermath. She couldn't help but feel a bit exposed to his frank, assessing gaze in those moments of intense quiet, yet she couldn't summon the will to object or do anything about it.

After long moments of shared heated breaths, he finally nodded his satisfaction. "I think I did more than loosen your lips."

She had to laugh, despite being flustered. "Understatement of the year."

"I take it you like kissing?" He swiveled to face her, propping an arm along the back of the cream-colored vinyl seat, his fingers toying with her hair.

A residual shiver tripped over her at his touch.

"I've never liked it *that* much before." She straightened her floral skirt to cover up a little more thigh, her fingers still trembling just a little. "That was a definite first for me."

"Really?" He flashed her an all-male smile, at once possessive and full of pride. "Must have been a hell of a kiss."

"It might have been partly the rocking of the boat, too." Her cheeks heated a little at the open acknowledgement of what had just happened, but she couldn't very well let him think she was the kind of woman who came apart at the brush of a man's lips.

Far from it.

She'd had sex before that hadn't been as... fulfilling...as Seth's kiss.

His smile slipped. "The rocking of the boat?"

"Well, partly." She tried to shrug off the awkwardness of the moment, looking out across the vast expanse of open water, no land in any direction. She gathered her courage, determined to be bold for a change. She tried to imagine what her mother might say to a man in this situation. "Is it just me, or is that rocking kind of an erotic movement?"

Granted, she had been a closet sensualist for most of her life. She had never been as good a sculptor as she was a painter, but she still sculpted because she loved the slide of wet clay over her palms, the twirl of a half-formed object coming to life in her hands.

She dreamed of one day planting a huge flower garden so she would have an excuse to play in the dirt, to absorb the rich scents of damp earth, blooming jasmine and honeysuckle.

So maybe she was unique in her enjoyment of a rocking boat. She stared at Seth as he grew quiet, perhaps concentrating on the gentle undulation of water beneath them.

For a moment, he stared into her eyes. As a small wave swayed the cruiser, lifting them up and back down in their seats, a current of pure electricity sizzled between them, connecting them in a mutual thought, a mutual feeling.

"Holy hell." Seth shot to his feet, gripping the windshield of the helm to brace himself for the sudden move.

"You see what I mean?"

"Yeah, I see exactly what you mean and thanks for ruining my fishing trips for the next fifty years." He swiped a hand through his spiky brown hair, leaving the strands standing up even straighter than before. "We'd better get out of here before we start going down a dangerous path."

She rose, insinuating herself between him and the boat's ignition. "Dangerous" sounded like exactly what she needed. Hadn't she been hiding from taking chances for too long already? No way was she going back to Twin Palms without the assurance that she could take a few risks now and then.

"But that's exactly where I want to go." She'd signed on for adventure, damn it. She'd never find it if they stuck to Seth's predetermined plan of tourist fun for the day.

Her mother wouldn't settle for that if *she* was looking for adventure. This week, neither would Mia. She flashed him her best flirtatious smile and beckoned him closer.

"Why don't you show me the rest of your boat?"

SHE MIGHT as well have asked to see his etchings. Seth knew exactly where she was headed with this "show-me-your-boat" business, and he wasn't so sure he should go there.

He barely knew Mia. And although he'd dated plenty of women, he'd never dated a woman he didn't know well. Maybe some he'd only known a brief time chronologically, but he always understood their *type*—sophisticated, fast-track, know-the-score women who were as upwardly mobile and ambitious as him.

Mia didn't fit into any type he recognized. A self-confessed sensualist artist who didn't hesitate to kidnap a pirate and cause a big scene. Yet she balked at the idea of being on television, even if it might help her career.

And, God help him, she could come undone in his arms with just a kiss. He was still battling the surge of lust he'd felt at seeing her fly apart.

But no matter how overtly enticing she might be, or how much she might say she just wanted a little adventure in her life, Seth had the feeling sex with Mia wouldn't be the kind of thing he could just walk away from. He'd known her for a couple of hours and already he felt mesmerized by those big green eyes of hers. The contradiction of her sensual nature and her forward way of speaking proved an appealing puzzle.

"I just don't think it's a good idea to see the rest of the boat." He reached for the ignition but Mia shifted her hip in his path.

He drew his hand back, knowing if he touched her once more, he wouldn't be able to stop touching her.

"Why not?" She peered around the deck until her gaze landed on the stairs leading to the berth.

"Because there's a bed down there, Mia. A big bed in a tiny cabin." Was he the dumbest guy on earth to forsake a chance at having this sexiest-of-all female in that bed? Or was he being smart to save himself messy complications with a woman he'd probably never understand?

He plowed ahead, hoping he fell into the latter category. "And I don't think it's such a good idea to go traipsing down there next to that big bed when we're both already thinking about orgasms and sex and...undulation."

A breeze tossed her dark hair over her shoulder, sending the silky strands to wave, flaglike, behind her. She smiled, a small upturn of her lips that called to mind illicit kisses and all the things a sensualist sort of woman might do with her mouth.

"You make it sound like a dirty word," she chastened.

"No, you make it sound like a sexy-as-hell word when it shouldn't be." He'd probably get an erection for the rest of his life when he heard someone say "undulate." Lucky for him, it wasn't the kind of thing apt to surface in daily conversation, right?

She edged by him, her gaze focused on the stairs behind the helm.

"Wait a minute." He scrambled after her, her floral skirt flapping in the breeze and teasing him with glimpses of thigh. "Where are you going?"

"I just want to look around. You don't need to come with me." Mia gripped the handrail at the head of the stairs and started down, puckering her lips at him to pantomime an exaggerated kiss before she totally disappeared. "Although you might have fun if you let yourself."

No other man with even a flicker of a pulse would ignore such a blatant invitation. But damn it, he didn't get involved in relationships lightly. Never had. Never would.

His father's lack of commitment to his family had taught Seth from an early age to be responsible, to take care of everyone around him, and most of all, not to get involved with any woman on the spur of the moment to assuage some temporary hunger.

Seth had only just taken his boat out of storage last weekend, and he sure as hell didn't have any condoms lying around for protection's sake. No way was he getting into a situation he couldn't control, even if the woman in question had him wound so tight he couldn't see straight.

"Wow! You call this tiny?" Mia enthused from downstairs, her thin sandals padding around the hardwood floors below deck. "This is huge!"

Her compliment nudged him closer to the stairwell.

He'd always loved this dang boat. The cruiser had been his first totally selfish purchase once he'd had enough money to do as he pleased. Now he could afford a boat that would make this one look like an afterthought, but Seth would sooner part with his corner office with a Bay view or his fifty-yard line season tickets for Buccaneers games before he traded in his boat.

How could he not go downstairs to sing its praises when Mia was so obviously interested? He could take ten minutes to show her the boat and then they'd be on their way to a routine tourist trek to Egmont Key.

Besides, it wasn't like Mia was going to jump him, right?

He took the stairs two at a time and realized by the time he got to the bottom that his body seemed to be in charge here and his rational mind was in danger of being utterly ignored. Knowing that didn't stop his feet from finding their way to Mia.

She stood in the salon, turning her head every which way and running her palm across the surface of an interior wall.

When she noticed him, she pointed toward the porthole. "The light is great in here. See how that last little bit of sunset casts a pinkish glow on this wall? You need a strip of mural right here to soak up the colors."

He envisioned a painting of a big fish on the wall. "How about a guy wrestling an oversize dolphin fish?"

She frowned. "I was seeing more of a quiet tropical island, but I guess that would work."

"You want the tour?"

Nodding, she joined him, taking his arm so he could lead her through the cabin areas. He started with the master stateroom so he could get it over with first. The double bed seemed much bigger than that in the small space. A navy comforter and white pillows made the room inviting, and Seth braced himself to be enticed by Carmen the Temptress.

"Nice," Mia commented, taking it all in before she backed into another room. "And this is the kitchen?"

"Galley," he corrected automatically, surprised at the twinge of disappointment he experienced at not being wrestled onto the bed. He reached into the chest of drawers in his stateroom and found a T-shirt to wear, then joined her in the kitchen. "I'm not much of a chef, but then, it doesn't take much talent to make fresh fish taste good."

"So this boat belongs to you, not the bank?" Mia ran her fingers over the countertops, clicking out a quick rhythm with her nails on the laminated surface.

Of course, she thought he worked for Gulf Coast. Part-time pirate and full-time gopher. How the hell could he have ever afforded a toy like this on a pirate's wages?

"Yeah. I bought it a few years ago with some money I'd been saving." Not an outright lie. Still, he hustled to redirect her as he pulled his T-shirt over his head. "But I spend a lot of time on the water, so it seemed worth it. You probably don't think twice about how much you spend on paints and canvas."

She followed him toward the guest stateroom, a cabin rich with red woods and burgundy linens. "Painting is a lot cheaper than sculpting at least. Clay is reasonable, but if you want to work in stone, you can go into debt in no time. Especially if you mess up and need to start over again."

Drifting toward the stairs, Mia seemed to be finished with the tour. And she hadn't even tried to talk him into a torrid coupling on the double bed.

Well, damn.

Before he could consider the consequence of the action, he reached out to grip one arm, lightly holding her still. "Wait, Mia."

She pivoted to face him, her straight brown hair blowing in the breeze wafting down from the deck. "Hmm?"

Now that he had her attention, he had to scavenge for his thoughts. His mind kept flashing back to that moment on the helm seat when she'd lost herself in a world of sensation. The moment her head had tipped back and...

"Seth?"

Her eyes were sharply focused now as she stared into his, waiting for him to speak.

"We never got a chance to talk more after what happened on deck...."

She closed her eyes, and for a moment, Seth thought perhaps he'd embarrassed her by bringing it up. But then, she opened her eyes again and blurted, "The orgasm incident?"

"That's the one." The woman didn't mince words. "But I thought maybe you'd be willing to talk to me now, maybe tell me why you won't go back for the press interview tonight."

"Why? Are you going to try to coerce me into going anyway?"

She not only didn't mince words, she obviously didn't pull punches either.

He shrugged. "I hear the bank shells out a lot of money to sponsor Gasparilla. Part of my job is to create good P.R., and to make sure you have a good time today. But it seems like I can't possibly do both. You're not going to have a good time if you have to give the bank any more publicity, right?"

"It's not that I don't want to give back to the bank." She sighed, leaned a shoulder against the doorframe around the stairs. "I just have a family with very old-fashioned values who will promptly go into cardiac arrest if they see me on TV with a half-dressed pirate talking about my day in captivity."

A wave rocked the boat, reminding Seth of undulating and other things he shouldn't be thinking about right now. He tugged her by the hand toward the salon, hoping if they took a seat they wouldn't feel the rocking of the damn boat quite so much.

"That probably sounds like the hang-up of some college kid," she continued as she followed him, dutifully sinking into the curved, green leather sofa. "But honestly, my grandparents are getting up there in years and I swear my granddad's ulcers get worse with every guy I date."

Seth nodded, understanding all too well the need to put family first. He flicked the lights on the lowest setting and slid into the seat next to her, careful to leave a few feet between them. No sense tempting fate. "You're close to your grandparents?"

"They pretty much raised me. My mom is single and she's never really gotten it through her head that having a child requires some stability. I adore my mom, but we're more like sisters than mother and daughter.'' She toyed with the fringe on her skirt for a moment, lost in thought. Then, as if remembering he was there, she crossed her legs and flipped her hair over one shoulder. ''But I did *not* jump into your arms today so we could discuss my family. I thought maybe you called me back here because you were ready to try out the bed now.''

''You're concerned about your grandfather's ulcers, yet you would sacrifice yourself to a pirate's lust for the sake of adventure?'' Sounded damn good to him, even if he didn't want to admit it. He had to give her credit for openness and honesty. The woman didn't know the meaning of the word coy. ''Have you considered that maybe your granddad worries himself sick for a good reason?''

''Not a chance. Face it, Chandler. *You'd* be sacrificing yourself to my *lust,* and no one but us has to know.'' She kicked her sandaled foot in a slow, circular rhythm. ''So what do you say? Are you game?''

Was he game? Hell, maybe he should tear a page from her book and take things a little less seriously. He knew he couldn't afford to try out the bed for real. But if he viewed this more in terms of a three-strikes-and-you're-out sort of game, he ought to be able to kiss her one more time without losing control completely.

And he deserved that kiss after the day he'd been having. He'd had to fend off a costumer who'd tried to talk him into wearing a hook on his hand, and ended up submitting to a tricorn hat he later tossed overboard. He suffered an eye patch for half a day and had paraded into town bare-chested and yo-ho-hoing.

No wonder pirates demanded a little booty for their trouble.

"I don't trust either of us near that bed, Mia, and with good reason." He settled his hand on her knee, allowing the heat of his palm to penetrate the cool silk of her skin. "But I know another game you might enjoy."

MIA WONDERED if it was possible to melt at a man's touch. If so, she stood a very good chance of pooling at Seth's feet any moment because his hand on her knee made her whole body turn warm and liquid.

She'd been so hell-bent determined to attract his attention, to make him waver from his honorable, "hands-off" course, that she had no idea what to do once her plan started working.

And judging by the heated challenge in his eyes, it was working very well.

"Another game?" she managed to push past dry lips.

He walked his fingers up the outside of her thigh until his hand landed on her hip. Then he scooted her closer to him in the dimly lit salon. "It's called 'let's see if we can make lightning strike twice.'"

She was still processing what exactly that meant when he angled his lips over hers. Realization hit at the same time he cupped her cheek in his palm and tilted her mouth for a deeper taste.

The man planned to drug her with his aphrodisiac kisses and then coax her right into orgasmic heaven.

All of which sounded delightful, except...

"That's not fair to you." Mia broke off their kiss, much to her lips' regret. Heat simmered between them, fogging the porthole windowpane behind them.

Seth flexed his fingers on her hip, caressed the curve of her waist with the broad expanse of his palm. "It's perfectly fair," he whispered, leaning forward to reclaim her mouth.

She shook her head, refusing him in spite of the persuasive press of his chest against hers. "No, I think you'd better let me pay you back first."

He stared at her through lazy brown eyes. "Honey, I can't think of anything I'd like more than to watch those waves roll right over you again, to see your mouth fall open and your head tip back when you—"

"No." Sensing the need to take action before he had her talked into becoming erotically dependent on him, Mia walked her fingers down his chest to the waistband of his khaki shorts. "I can think of something you would definitely like more."

His abs flexed under her touch. He tensed, his whole body going still as she continued a relentless path down his shorts toward the ridge she spied very clearly.

She didn't know where she found the nerve. Maybe too many nights of longing for adventure, of promising herself she'd take advantage of this trip away from home, had conspired to mold her into this wild woman.

Gathering her courage, she smoothed her hand over that ridge and looked him in the eye.

''I bet I send you into orbit without ever hitting the sheets.''

4

A MAN COULD PASS OUT over that kind of invitation.

Seth knew this firsthand, because Mia's erotic proposal sent every drop of his blood on a heated southbound tidal wave, leaving him damn near lightheaded and too turned-on to think straight.

All he had to do was nod.

Instead, some dying part of his conscience rasped out a gravelly, "What?"

Mia's hand curled around him, assuring him he'd understood the message. "Payback can be very satisfying."

There could be no mistaking how much he wanted to. She couldn't help but realize the full extent of his hunger for her.

Unfortunately, something about the word "payback" on her lips niggled his numbed brain cells, reminding him that he expected more from his relationships than just an even exchange of pleasure.

Cursed principles.

He edged away from her, prying himself up off the couch. Was it his imagination, or was there a hint of disappointment in her eyes that went beyond sexual frustration? "I'd give my eyeteeth to take you up on that offer, Mia, but I made a promise to myself a long time ago not to indulge in this kind of thing lightly.''

She bit her lip, broadcasting an uncertainty he hadn't expected from her. ''I guess I misinterpreted your kiss. I thought you wanted this, too.''

The flash of self-doubt in her eyes lashed at his stupid conscience, making him feel like a total heel.

''I do want this, Mia. I want it so much it's damned well about to kill me.'' Still, he backed up a step as he said it, knowing if he let himself get too close to her again, any promises from his past would be incinerated to ashes. ''I just didn't plan for this and I don't have any way to protect you....'' He'd be lying if he let her think that was the only reason why. She didn't even know his true identity. ''But mostly I just don't let myself get involved with any woman I'm not fully committed to.''

Assuming a live-in relationship constituted a full commitment, anyway. He wasn't his father, damn it. At least he offered something beyond sex to the women he slept with.

Her mouth curved into a perfectly round *O* though no sound came forth. Her cheeks tinged pink for a few seconds, confirming his fear that he'd embarrassed her.

''You've got to know it's not you,'' he rushed to assure her, guilt nipping at his heels. ''Hell, look at me. I'm a walking advertisement for how much I'd like to take you up on that offer.''

Her green eyes slid downward to linger just below his waist.

His temperature spiked a few more degrees, making him wonder why he found it necessary to reassure a woman who was leading him around by the...nose.

A slow smile curled her lips, her feminine pride apparently soothed by his obvious arousal. "Then I suppose the polite thing for me to do would be to leave you alone so I don't tempt you any further."

His wayward libido already protested the move. "That would be helpful, yes."

"Okay." Her green cat eyes met his again, alight with mischief. "I'll let you go about your business and I'll go about mine as if you weren't even here."

He nodded, half-hating that plan, but knowing his promise not to get involved with any woman on a casual basis wouldn't survive the rest of the trip without her cooperation.

"Okay, then." He backed himself right into the staircase, his heel colliding with the first step. "I'd better start up the boat and get us underway again. It's too dark to see much of anything on the island now, but we can at least circle the key before we head back to Gasparilla."

She nodded a bit too agreeably. How could she be taking this so well when his body cursed volumes at him?

"Okay. If you don't mind, I'll go up on deck too, but I promise to sit on the other side of the boat."

He was about to tell her that wasn't necessary, but judging from the way his pulse kicked into overdrive at her approach, she was probably better off out of reach.

"Of course." He turned to take the stairs two at

a time. "It's a great night to see the stars," he called to her as he hit the deck. Maybe a little sky gazing would keep them both distracted.

"Don't worry about me," she replied, heading for the bow while he slid into the helm seat. "I don't even know you're here."

Seth frowned, his ego taking another hit that she could write him off with such ease. He should be patting himself on the back that he'd averted a crisis, but instead, he could only think about how much he'd cost himself by rejecting Mia's tantalizing offer.

With an oath, he turned the key in the boat's ignition, dragging his gaze from her curvy silhouette outlined in moonlight.

Lost in the contemplation of those curves, it took Seth a minute to realize that noting had happened when he'd turned the key. No throaty growl of twin engines greeted his ears. The only sound he could hear was the incessant undulation of waves against the boat.

Damn. Damn. Damn.

He clicked off the ignition and tried again.

Nothing.

Recognition slid over him. This had happened to him once before, his first year with the boat. After keeping a vessel in storage, sometimes condensation could flood the fuel cell and corrupt both engines. No doubt, that accounted for the silence, the darkness on the water.

A silence broken only by the smooth lap of the waves. A darkness interrupted only by the outline of sexy Mia Quentin slowly peeling off her skirt.

No SELF-RESPECTING Floridian would ever dream of jumping into the middle of the Gulf in February. Spring Breakers and snowbirds didn't mind, but she wouldn't normally venture so much as a toe in the surf until at least April.

Thing is, she was smarting just a little from Seth's continued rejection. She'd put so much effort into today's pirate seduction that she couldn't imagine returning to endless days of hawking seashell necklaces in Twin Palms without at least making it to second base with her quarry.

What more could she do to capture the man's attention, other than rip off her clothes? As a final resort she was willing to fake the urge for an evening swim. In truth, she didn't want to get anywhere near that water. Not only because of the cold, but because she knew better than to swim in strange waters at night.

But *he* didn't have to know that.

She had the feeling she'd succeeded in catching his eye when a strangled expletive shot across the deck.

"What in the hell do you think you're doing?" Seth stormed right across the bow right behind his words.

Mia's skirt already lay pooled at her feet. Her silk blouse just barely covered the red lace bikini bottoms that looked more like panties than swimwear.

"I thought I'd go for a dip to clear my head once we get to the shallow waters around Egmont Key." She hoped he wouldn't notice the goose bumps populating both her bare legs.

"A dip?" He reached for her sarong and held it in between them like a shield. "Jesus, woman, are you crazy? There could be sharks in there for all you know."

She hoped the dark would hide the blood blanching right out of her face. She hadn't even thought of the sharks. But did he have to stare at her like she'd just lost her mind along with half her outfit?

Reaching for the hem of her shirt, she flashed him what she hoped was a nonchalant smile. "Then maybe I'll settle for letting the back spray of the water cool me off once we get underway again."

With a quick prayer for a little more nerve to carry her through, Mia whipped the silk blouse over her head and flung it into the night breeze.

Seth didn't look turned on so much as he looked like he'd just swallowed a frog or something equally uncomfortable. She wondered if she'd overestimated her appeal in this high-octane, red lace swimsuit and cursed herself for dropping three figures on a getup she'd most likely never wear again.

She could have had an all-out spree at the art supply store for what she'd spent.

By now, Mia only wished she could crawl back into her clothes and forget her stupid wish for adventure. Seth's expression remained as horrified as if she'd told him he had to walk the plank. His lips moved, but so far, no sound issued forth from his mouth.

"Put. This. On." Finally, he eked out that much, handing her the sarong.

Defeated, she yanked the gauzy floral fabric out

of his hand and shook out the wrinkles. "Fine. I will. But you were supposed to pretend I wasn't even here, remember?"

"I could scarcely function when you had your clothes *on*. I'm supposed to ignore you when you're almost naked?"

Despite the fact that he was practically yelling at her, Mia's mood improved considerably. Maybe her efforts hadn't been wasted after all.

"Sorry." She wrapped the sarong around her waist and tied the knot with slow deliberation. "I thought you were going to be concentrating on driving the boat and you wouldn't even notice me."

His gaze narrowed, communicating his suspicion quite effectively. Still, he didn't comment on her blatant lie. "That's where we have a little problem."

"We do?"

"The boat won't start." The grimace on his face made him look dangerous enough to sport the eye patch and dagger he'd long ago ditched.

Mia realized she didn't experience the slightest qualm at the thought of being stuck out here alone with Seth, however. After seeing him play noble with her one too many times tonight, she figured he must be a pretty upstanding, trustworthy guy.

"The boat won't start? It sounds like a tried and true ploy to fool around with your date." She sidled closer, just in case Seth had changed his mind about testing out the bed below deck. "Remember on *Happy Days* when Richie would conveniently run out of gas so he could score with his girlfriend?"

"Do you think that's what I'm doing? Not starting

up my boat to angle for more time with you when I've just admitted you've got me tied up in so many damned knots I can't think straight?'' The rippling water below them cast constantly moving shadows over Seth's face. The moonlight that would have seemed pale on dry land now lit their whole world.

"Spoilsport.'' Mia shivered and tried to hide it. If ever she'd been worried she'd inherited her mother's wild ways with men, Seth's reaction to her tonight had put that fear to rest in a hurry. "Care to at least tell me how we're going to get home then?''

Seth's jaw clenched as he bent to pick up her blouse off the deck. "I'm sure we could signal someone for a tow, but if you don't mind waiting a little longer to be rescued, I'd prefer to have my uncle come get us. He'll be able to fix the boat tomorrow if I can get it to him tonight.'' He handed her the shirt, keeping his eyes trained on her face.

"I'm in no hurry.'' She shrugged into the halter top, disappointed to see Seth pulling a cell phone out of his pants pocket rather than watching her. "Even though you're determined to thwart all my adventures, at least I'm getting to spend some time out on the water tonight. That's sort of fun.'' She couldn't remember the last time she'd been on a boat. She didn't own one, and she would never rent one given her run-ins with Frankie the marina guy.

"Sorry about this, Mia.'' He started punching numbers into the keypad, pointing the antenna back toward St. Petersburg.

"Not a problem.'' Time to grow up and pack away her fantasy. "I should be thanking you instead of trying to lead you astray. This is more adventure than I've had in ages.''

He rolled his eyes. ''We'll see if you're still saying that after you've been stuck out here another hour and—'' He held up his finger as he listened to whatever was going on at the other end of his phone call, then spoke into the receiver. ''Hey Uncle Brock, it's Seth…''

Mia slipped away from his conversation and headed toward the back of the boat, unwilling to cause the guy any more grief tonight. She wasn't sure whether to applaud his noble efforts not to dally with a woman he wasn't seeing, or to curse his incredible restraint for not making a move on her since the oh-so-startling orgasm incident.

The night air held a slight chill, but not enough to give her goose bumps even without Seth next to her. She smoothed her hands up and down her bare arms, wishing for Seth's touch instead of her own.

Why hadn't she paid more attention to her mother's seductive moves around men? Maybe she'd be rolling around in the pirate's cabin being treated to a mind-blowing ravishing instead of haunting the shadows while Seth tied up the details with his uncle.

But she'd given it her best shot, damn it. She didn't want a relationship in her life—she'd seen firsthand from her mother how men could distort a woman's priorities and make her forget what was important in life.

She'd only wanted a weekend to play, and somehow she had managed to get herself kidnapped by a sexy pirate. Even if the story ended right there, it was more excitement than she'd been treated to since her mother had surprised her with an offer to work a few hours in the tourist shop last week.

Of course, tonight's adventure would be just as fleeting as that offer would probably turn out to be.

Mia just wasn't the kind of woman to live on the edge, and sooner or later she was going to have to resign herself to that. She was going to leave Seth far behind once they hit dry land.

Right after she stole one more kiss.

SETH WAITED as long as he could to approach her. He'd tried calling his brother umpteen times to discuss the boat problems but got no answer. He'd checked and double-checked the engines, hoping he overlooked some glitch in the mechanics he could fix after all.

Now, he couldn't put off spending a few more minutes with her before his uncle arrived. He was supposed to be showing her a good time tonight. Instead he'd spent the entire night running from her.

He regarded Mia sprawled out along the cushions at the back of the boat. She lay on one side, propped on an elbow and looking out over the moonlit water.

Her resemblance to Carmen had faded since she'd lost her flower and she no longer flaunted her very appealing self in front of him. Now, her long hair trailed down over her shoulders and snaked around her body at intriguing intervals.

She gave the impression of a sea nymph washed up out of the water, and Seth suddenly envisioned exactly what he wanted painted on that blank wall below deck. *Her.* Irrepressible Mia Quentin, possibly clad in nothing but red lace.

He'd barely recovered from that most recent assault on his senses. He was lucky he hadn't gone into cardiac arrest at that little stunt.

He'd dated his share of beautiful women. But they all sort of blended together in his memory now, a chain of failed relationships with women who'd been all wrong for him, women who left citing the same catalog of his shortcomings.

Of course, the possibility loomed that he sucked at relationships and that every one of those women had been right. Given his high rate of failure, that seemed fairly likely.

But maybe, just maybe, he'd made a mistake in choosing the kinds of women to get involved with. One day, instead of finding women who were as cynical about dating as him, he would be with someone more passionate, someone who hadn't lost her sense of optimism for romance.

Someone like Mia.

The idea teased the edges of his brain, tempting him with a mental picture every bit as enticing as the one of Mia in red lace. He'd been running from her because he didn't get involved with any woman lightly. But what if he initiated something more committed with Mia? Would she go for a relationship, or was she such a wild child that one-night encounters and pirate abductions were more her speed?

Too bad he'd started the night off by lying to her about his ties to the Gasparilla fest. Would she resent his evasion of the truth? Or would she be all the more tempted to give up her wild child ways if she knew his bottom line?

The thought grated.

"Are you going to join me, Blackbeard, or am I going to have to stargaze by myself all night?" Mia twisted on the cushions to glance back at him, her smile beckoning him.

Damn it. He wanted her. Wanted more from her than just this night. But telling her who he was might irrevocably shift their relationship into the same territory that always got him into trouble with women. He never knew if they wanted him for himself.

"Come on, Chandler. I promise I won't bite." Mia sat up and patted the vacated space beside her. "This time, anyway."

Seth weighed his options as he moved closer. Edgy from wanting this woman, he couldn't afford to make rash decisions based on sexual attraction. He would feel out the situation a bit, maybe get a handle on how receptive she would be to exploring things a little more slowly.

Mia folded her arms and propped her feet on the low rail ringing the edge of the deck. "I don't suppose you came over here for one last kiss?"

He slid into place beside her, wondering how *he* could ever move slowly, even if he could convince *her* they should take their time. "That depends. What if I didn't want this to be the last kiss, but the first of many more?"

She lifted one delicate brow in surprise. "I think I made it perfectly clear I was willing to engage in the sensual activities of your choice tonight." She started to smile, but midway up, her lips did a U-turn, curving into a definite frown. "But don't you think your uncle will be arriving soon?"

It took him a minute to recover from thinking about the sensual activity of his choice. "That's not what I meant. I was thinking more along the lines of one kiss tonight, and another kiss tomorrow. Maybe a few more next weekend."

Her frown downgraded to an outright scowl. He wouldn't have thought the woman who had practically jumped him two hours ago could all but recoil in horror from him now.

"Are you implying we should see each other again?"

"Don't you think that's a more natural progression after a few shared kisses than fast forwarding straight to sheet tangling?"

"No!" She blurted the word, but blushed in its aftermath. "I mean, maybe for some people that's a reasonable way to go about things, but I'm not in the market for a relationship right now."

Didn't women always want to be in a relationship? Seth had never encountered any problems selling women on monogamy before. But then, he'd never met a woman as wild and willing as Mia.

The idea that she would turn him down niggled the competitive streak in him. His stubborn refusal to lose had cemented his rise to the top of his profession.

And damn it, he didn't want her trying out all that wild and willing energy on anyone but him.

"Why not? You have more pirates to run off with next week?"

She hugged her knees to her body, green eyes fixed at a point far out in the water. "I have to get back to real life next week. That means no more pirates, pleasure cruises or undulating. I've got a business to run, a dysfunctional family to manage and about ten doctors' appointments to drag my grandparents to. Besides, even if Grandpa didn't go into a downward health spiral every time a man came near me, I would be too mired in work to sneak in any kisses next weekend." She tipped her head sideways to glance at him. "Thanks for offering though. It helps soothe my stinging feminine pride a bit to think you might have been interested if we'd had more time."

In the distance, Seth heard the whine of a boat engine. Several boats had passed them since they'd broken down, but none for the past ten minutes.

"We do have more time." If he was going to tell her the truth about his identity, the moment had arrived to do so, but something about the resolution in her voice made him hold his tongue.

"No, we don't." She released her knees to sit up straight in the seat beside him. Her gaze met his, serious and steady, lacking the playful mischief that had been there earlier in the evening. "We're all out of opportunities for anything but a good-night kiss."

She was turning him down?

Frustration hounded him, but didn't deter him. He'd have another chance with Mia Quentin, whether she knew it yet or not.

He would convince her to try out a relationship that had more to do with endless nights and multiple orgasms than quickie sex and stolen moments.

And the time to start his slow seduction was right now.

"Then I guess you'd better slide a little closer." Seth pulled her across the seat cushions and slid her right across his lap.

The thin fabric of her skirt did little to dull the sensation of her bottom on his thighs. He palmed the small of her back with one hand and curled the other about her neck to draw her lips down to his.

The drone of a boat motor closed in, filling his ears but not dissuading him from his purpose. He was going to make Carmen rethink her position on commitment with a kiss guaranteed to make her remember who her ravisher was today.

And who she wanted it to be in the future.

He whispered a kiss across her mouth, teasing her lips with the warmth of his breath and the cool of the night air. She shivered, a tiny whimper catching at the back of her throat.

Keying into that moment of weakness, that small sign of desire, Seth angled his lips a bit more sharply over hers and slid his tongue between her teeth, his first act of possessiveness all day. Mia slid her arms around his shoulders, pressed herself tighter to him.

The ensuing sense of affirmation made him all the more sure of his plan. He dipped her backward to the bench seat behind her, and followed her down with his own body. For a moment he held her there, allowing her to feel his weight against her, giving her time to absorb the heat of him.

If he hadn't been so determined to give her a brief taste of her own teasing medicine, Seth would have lost all control right then and there. She arched ever so slightly into him, wriggling her way closer until he thought he'd lose it if he didn't peel off all her clothes and take her now.

For a guy so well in control, it sure as hell was difficult to pry himself back off her. She smelled like flowers and she tasted good enough to—

A spotlight flashed across them, ringing them in a sudden blinding circle.

"All hands on deck, Seth," an obnoxious male voice shouted through a bullhorn from somewhere out on the water. "Even the ones you're using to maul that pretty girl. Your savior has arrived."

Mia almost jumped out of her skin in her rush to sit up now that a forty-foot fishing boat floated a few yards away from them.

Some savior. Seth had been halfway to heaven on one mind-drugging kiss when Uncle Brock had to make a typically raucous entrance.

Getting hauled back to Tampa behind Brock's boat would definitely douse Seth's provocative plans for Mia tonight, but he was a man on a mission now. Even if he had to follow Mia back to Small Town, U.S.A. to convince her to give a relationship a try, Seth had every intention of reclaiming those lips.

5

MIA TRACED a finger over her lips, remembering
Seth's heated kiss as she stared absently at a post-
modern painting on display in the Tampa Museum
of Art's permanent exhibition.

She'd taken a tour of the museum to try and divert
her thoughts from Seth Chandler, but so far, she'd
failed miserably. Her daydreams had mentally
painted his face on all the male statues in the antiquities section. Even now, as she stared at a dark
painting full of enigmatic images, Mia's mind took
an erotic turn when she spied the title—*The Voyeur.*

She wouldn't mind a peep show if her wicked pirate happened to be the main attraction. Their time
together Saturday night had ended much too quickly
when Seth's uncle had shown up. The shouting
through the bullhorn had almost scared her straight
out of her sarong.

Brock Chandler had turned out to be a nice enough
guy, if a little gruff around the edges. He'd towed
Seth's boat back to his place for repair and then he'd
given them both a ride home. Not the most romantic
way to end a day that had started out with such sizzling promise, but Mia had to admit she'd had fun.

It could have been a great start to a relationship if

she wasn't in the midst of professional and family crises at every turn. As it was, she'd kissed Seth good-night—quickly, in light of their audience—with more than a little regret.

At least she'd managed to bypass the stint on the eleven o'clock news. One newscast a day was plenty, thank you very much.

She looked back up at *The Voyeur* and wondered what had happened to her determined effort to see a man naked this weekend. The fact that she had to fulfill this wish with a trip to an art museum ranked as majorly pathetic.

Even so, she was contemplating one more swing through the antiquities section for a final peek before she tackled her 3:00 p.m. meeting with the bank when her cell phone shook her purse with silent vibrations.

Mia dug in her bag as she skirted away from the museum goers, finding relative privacy at a window overlooking the Hillsborough River.

"Hello?" Her heart jumped as she waited for the caller to speak. She'd given the number strictly to family members as she always worried about her grandfather.

"I've got a double Master's from a prestigious university," Noelle Quentin launched into conversation without preamble, "and I have no flipping clue how to operate the cash register."

Mia sighed. "Hello, Mom."

"Mia, I'm trying so hard to cover for you at the store, but it's impossible with your grandfather boring holes into my back with the I-told-you-so look.

What do I do when the whole computer system locks up and I just get an annoying error message?'' In the background, Mia could hear her mother jamming computer keys and the computer beeping back at her.

''Don't get Grandpa upset Mom, you know that's not good for his ulcer.'' She stared out the window to the Moorish spires of the University of Tampa, wondering if she'd ever be able to escape Twin Palms for more than a weekend.

''That belly-aching thing he does is not an ulcer, Mia, it's called emotional manipulation and the man is an expert from way back.''

Mia could practically hear poor Grandpa's belly roiling. She adored her grandparents, but they had never fully recovered from the feared social stigma of their daughter having a baby at age sixteen. They'd raised Mia as their own, insisting Noelle go off to college far away to be among people who wouldn't know her background.

Of course, everyone had known anyway because Noelle had never been ashamed of her situation or her daughter for so much as a minute.

''Mom—''

''I promise to be nice to your grandfather and load him up with antacids if you will please make this damn message go away.''

''Hit escape,'' Mia hissed into the phone, frustrated that she'd set aside her sexy daydreams to play counselor to her dysfunctional family.

Through the magic of cellular technology, Mia heard the distinct hum of an efficient computer printing out a cash receipt.

"You're brilliant," Noelle announced. "Of course, you are *my* daughter. Have a great time in Tampa, Mia, and don't worry about a thing. We're all doing fine here. Smooches!"

Mia stared down at a phone gone dead.

If they were all doing so fine, why was the computer jammed and Grandpa gulping ulcer medicine? Obviously, she needed to get the mortgage ironed out at the bank and make tracks for home as soon as possible. If that meant putting more distance between her and the man she'd been thinking about all day, the man she'd dreamt about the past two nights, than so be it.

Dysfunctional or not, family came first.

Like a modern Cinderella, her time for fantasies had vanished at midnight. And a girl couldn't get much further from fairy tales than a trip to Gulf Coast Bank for a meeting with her loan officer.

"I'VE GOT A management meeting at the bank in half an hour, Brock, you think you could nudge this old boat any faster?" Seth glowered down at the still waters of the Hillsborough River, trying to discern if they were moving forward at all in Brock's ancient fishing boat.

"You know the rules in this stretch of the waterway. No wake." Not that Brock appeared to mind a bit as he steered through the channel, taking in the sights of downtown Tampa. "What's the matter, city boy? You've been jumping around like a fresh fish on deck all damn day."

That's because Seth hadn't particularly wanted to

go fishing with his uncle this afternoon, not when he had Mia Quentin on the brain. But he needed a favor from Brock, and there was no better way to warm him up to Seth's plan than by indulging the man's favorite sport for a few hours.

Brock might have been born a much younger brother to Seth's absentee father, but he had proven himself to be more like family than Seth's dad ever had. Brock was the older brother Seth never had, a wise counselor in the form of a very slow tour boat guide.

"I need your help."

"Twice in one week? This must be a record for you." Brock sipped his third iced coffee of the afternoon and cut the engines down another notch as Gulf Coast Bank finally came into view.

"I need you to help me find Mia."

"You lost her?"

"She checked out of her hotel this morning before I could find out where she lives." He didn't mention that Mia hadn't returned his calls from the day before, however. Seth drummed his thumbs in an impatient rhythm against the brass rail surrounding the bow, staring out at the sleek contemporary lines of the Tampa Museum of Art perched on the shore. "She may have been under the impression that I was only interested in a short-term relationship."

"Wise woman." Brock crumpled the paper cup his iced coffee had come in and shot the refuse into the wastebasket with a free-throw shot from ten feet out. "You've got a pisspoor record with the fair sex. No wonder she ran."

"Nice shot." Seth fought the urge to test his own aim from that far away. "What do you mean, piss poor record?"

Brock turned the wheel toward a docking area behind the bank's parking lot. "Any man who has had live-in relationships with, let's see, *five* different women has a record that would scare off any sane female."

"That's been over the past *ten* years." This conversation wasn't going at all as Seth had planned. Frustrated, he tore a piece of paper off a legal pad from his briefcase and crumpled it up. He lined up his shot and was about to follow through when an image of Mia in her swimsuit flitted across his brain at the last minute, sending his shot bouncing off the rim of the basket.

"Hell, at least I made a commitment to those relationships. I've never undertaken a relationship lightly, the way some Chandlers do."

Namely his brother, Jesse, and to a more harmful degree, his father.

"Don't look in my direction." Brock held up his hands in protest. "I'm too particular to have waded through as many women as you. And why do you need my help to find the one who got away, anyhow?"

Seth retrieved his paper to try again, heedless of the fact that they were now pulling up to the pier. He was going to make his shot and secure his favor, damn it.

"Why do you think I need your help? You spent eight years on the police force before you started making money off this boat of yours. Surely you know a thing or two about locating a person. She's not in the phonebook.'' A gust of wind carried the makeshift basketball to the left, ruining his aim.

Brock tied the boat to the moor with the quick efficiency of a man who'd lived on the water all his life. ''Maybe she doesn't want you to find her.''

''I'm going to change her mind.'' Seth had a quick, vivid vision of their shared kisses. ''Come on, Brock, cut me a break.''

Brock folded his arms across his chest, still sweaty from their afternoon of wrestling with fish. He tipped his head to one side, as if weighing the idea. ''You still making lots of money with my stocks?''

''You could buy a whole damn fleet of these boats with what I've got lined up for you.''

Brock nodded. ''Good man. It's Mia Quentin, right?''

''Yes.'' Scooping up the wadded ball of yellow paper one last time, Seth arced his shot straight into the basket. ''She's an artist.''

''Going cultural on me?'' Brock raised a brow.

''Sure. Right after I shower off the fish stink.'' Seth stepped onto the pier, briefcase in hand. ''I've got to hurry if I'm going make that meeting. Thanks, Brock.''

Kicking up his stride to an all-out run, Seth made a beeline for the ground-level gym facilities, confident Brock would find Mia. He needed a second chance to explore things more slowly with her, get to know her a little better.

And, of course, he had to come clean with her

about who he was and what he did for a living. But what woman wouldn't be secretly relieved to discover her pirate-bank gopher was actually two takeovers away from the Fortune 500 list?

Carmen was in for quite a surprise.

NO SURPRISES TODAY, Mia prayed as she waited in the bank's main floor lobby for her loan officer to see her.

People extended their loans all the time, right? She'd be fine once she sat down and actually started talking to the woman—Mia flipped the business card over in her hand to read the name again—Anna Beth Stanton. Anna Beth of Gulf Coast Bank. A division of Chandler Enterprises?

That last bit jumped out at Mia for the first time in her dealings with Gulf Coast, probably because the memory of a certain Seth Chandler had been tormenting her ever since she'd walked into her hotel room alone Saturday night.

An odd coincidence. Funny how sometimes when a person became aware of a new name or word, that name suddenly appeared all over the place. The city was probably full of Chandlers.

Of course, it was even funnier that she could swear she heard Seth's voice in the smooth baritone across the echoing marble bank lobby. A ridiculous notion, because a part-time pirate who did errands for the bank wouldn't be engrossed in a conversation about…she leaned back in her seat to hear more clearly…quarterly shareholder profits.

Still, the voice sounded so much like the one that

drifted through her daydreams, she couldn't resist swiveling in her chair to find the source.

Her gaze roamed the creamy Italian marble room and landed on Seth's clean-shaven twin dressed in a crisply tailored suit and a bright blue silk tie.

A far cry from her bare-chested Blackbeard with a dagger between his teeth.

Unbidden, her feet started in his direction.

"Seth?"

All talk of stock options ceased, making her realize she'd actually said his name aloud. She definitely hadn't meant to.

His eyes homed in on her, absorbed the sight of her as thoroughly as she'd been studying him.

It took a full three seconds before the light of recognition dawned in his eyes. She'd left her Carmen days far behind her now that she was dressed in a bland gray suit, her hair clipped neatly at the nape of her neck.

"Mia?" He walked away from his suit-clad companion, an older woman with a pinched expression and a gold nametag labeling her the bank manager.

She stalled in the middle of the lobby, allowing him to come to her, all the while drinking in his long-limbed stride, the way he smiled at her, the fluid movement of his body.

He grazed his hands over her arms before she'd totally admitted it must really be him. But once he touched her, once she caught a hint of his aftershave, once she absorbed the heat and nuances of his body right through the crisp lines of his suit, there could be no mistaking her pirate captor.

"I left a message for you yesterday," he started, searching her gaze with his own, "didn't you get it?"

Her mind worked overtime to process this new, Calvin Klein-attired Seth. She'd never expected to see him again, and she certainly hadn't expected this...stranger.

"I'm leaving town tonight," she blurted with zero grace. "I didn't call because I knew I wouldn't be able to get together." Her brain worked haltingly with his hands still lingering on her shoulders. But she couldn't keep her mouth in check. "What are you doing here? Dressed like this?"

She had a brief impression of Seth looking distinctly uncomfortable before a woman's voice called out across the lobby.

"Mia Quentin?" A young woman close to Mia's age stood in the doorway of an office, a file folder in her hand. "I'm ready to see you now."

Great. The most important appointment of her life and Mia was now completely flustered, muddle-headed and mute.

"She'll be there in a minute, Anna," Seth offered, placating the young woman with a smile while Mia backed away from him with feet that seemed awfully damned reluctant.

"No problem, Mr. Chandler." Anna shot Seth a warm smile before sauntering back toward her desk with a slow wiggle in her walk.

It took Mia at least ten seconds to pull her thoughts together and find her voice.

"Mr. Chandler." Her mind churned through what

she knew about him, hoping to find plausible explanations for the expensive suit and his lord-of-the-manor air, but came up empty. "You're obviously not the bank gopher, are you?"

"Why don't we have Anna reschedule your meeting and we can go talk—"

"You're Chandler Enterprises, aren't you?" She glanced down at the business card she still clutched in one hand, rereading Seth's name right there in black and white. "You own the bank?"

Why hadn't he just said so? Most guys would lie and say they owned the bank when they didn't own it. But then, most guys would have taken Mia up on her offer to play out an erotic abduction scenario, too. Yet Seth had pushed her away with both hands, even going so far as to let her believe he earned a living as a thirty-something errand boy.

"Not me, my company owns it." He put one hand around her back, as if to steer her out of the lobby. "But I can explain, if you'll just—"

"No need for explanations." Mia planted her heels on the slick marble floor. Did he honestly think she'd ever go anywhere with a man who would lie to her about something so basic? She didn't care how sexy he smelled, or how melt-in-your-mouth good he looked. She'd learned a long time ago not to get too attached to people who would only play games with her. "If you'll excuse me, I've got an appointment to keep."

Perhaps he heard the steel threaded through her words because his hand immediately fell away from her back. "At least give me a chance to talk to you when you're finished." He smoothed one hand down the length of his bright blue tie. "I don't want you to think I planned to deceive you, Mia. You sort of took me by surprise the other day."

She backed up another step, needing to put distance between them before she got trapped in more lies spun by a man who attracted her like the tide to the moon. What if he'd secretly been laughing at her paltry attempts at seduction?

"Of course. I flung myself at you and you were caught off guard." She backed right into her chair where her purse and her leather binder full of notes sat. She picked them up with slightly unsteady hands, folding them tightly in her arms. "No wonder you lied to me all day about who you were. Please, excuse me."

"I never meet people who don't know who I am, Mia." Seth followed her. Was he unaware of the bank full of curious stares behind him? "So when you didn't seem to recognize me—"

"Why should I have recognized you?" Mia shifted from flustered to flat out annoyed. "Were you *People* magazine's 'Sexiest Man of the Year' and I missed it?"

"I don't blame you for being angry." He appeared slightly chastened for all of two seconds before he slid one hand around her back as if to steer her toward the private offices down one corridor. "Why don't you tell me what business you have with the bank and I'll see if I can help you? I'm sure I can take care of things for you here, and maybe then you'll let me make it up to you?"

How many times had her mother's boyfriends promised to "take care of" something for Noelle? No way was Mia falling into the trap of depending on a man to pave the way in the world for her.

"I'm not going to discuss my business with someone I can't trust." She'd never be an independent businesswoman if she allowed someone like Seth to waltz into her world and wave a magic "I'm-the-boss" wand over her financial troubles.

He stiffened, insulted when he had no right to be, it seemed.

"Look, I'm not angry with you. But I don't need your help today, I just need to get into my meeting to iron out a few things with the bank." She took calming breaths, spoke in soothing tones, accustomed to dealing with her emotionally supercharged family. "Thanks for offering to make it up to me, but it's not necessary. I'm leaving town today as soon as my business is settled."

Seth's eyes narrowed, focusing solely on her. Despite the logical part of her brain telling her she needed to sever ties with this man, the not-so-logical part of her remembered his kiss, his touch, the havoc he could wreak on her body by brushing his against hers....

"Where are you headed?" He asked the question casually enough, but Mia had the impression he really wanted to know the answer. Was it her imagination, or could Seth Chandler be interested in her even after he'd pushed her away all day Saturday?

Unwilling to test her self-restraint by finding out, Mia hedged. "I'm going home. And right now, I really can't keep my appointment waiting any longer.'' She skirted past him and made a quick dash to the doorway of Anna's office. ''Bye, Seth.''

She hoped the fact that she flashed him a quick smile made up for the fact that she closed the door in his face.

Damn it, she didn't want to be attracted to a man who'd lied to her. And she definitely didn't want to be intrigued by the fact that he might really want her, even after he'd turned her down on Saturday.

She *had* to separate her tumultuous personal feelings from her professional need to secure an extension on the loan for the Quentin family's business. Bottom line, her family came first.

Mia had no time in her life for any man, let alone some power-tripping corporate tycoon. She wasn't about to let him in on her financial troubles, even if he did own the bank, of all things.

And she definitely had no intention of letting him close enough to play any of his games with her again.

6

HE WOULDN'T LET Mia slip away.

Although he made a cursory effort to plow through some paperwork in a vacated office he sometimes used on the main floor of the bank, Seth kept one eye trained on the door to Anna Stanton's office. Mia wouldn't leave the bank without him knowing. Without him on her tail.

When he finally heard the click of her high heels on the bare marble floor of the lobby, Seth sent his rolling chair flying across the office in his scramble to catch up with her.

"Mia!" he called out to her as she sailed through the double doors toward the parking lot. Her long hair, which had been formerly clipped into neat submission, now swung free down her back. The dark, shiny mass rippled in the breeze behind her as she headed for a tiny silver convertible that had seen better days.

Ready to ride out of his life.

Picking up the pace, Seth shoved through the doors and hightailed it across the pavement. "Mia, wait."

She paused in the process of unlocking the driver side door, her gray dress conservative in color even though the hemline fell appealingly short of her knees. "I think we said all we needed to say earlier."

She went back to unlocking her door, but Seth noticed her hands were a little less steady, her movements more awkward.

Wishful thinking to hope maybe she was remembering those kisses that had blown him out of the water the other night?

"Can I call you?"

"No." She opened the door and tossed a sheaf of papers in the passenger seat.

"Mia, I'm sorry about not coming clean Saturday." His fingers itched to touch her, to keep her from leaving. Even when his live-ins waltzed out his door, he couldn't remember wanting to stop them this badly.

But other than a sincere apology, what could he offer her?

She nodded reluctant acceptance of his words. "I guess we were both playing games this weekend. I shouldn't have coerced you into taking me captive either."

"I'm not playing games now." He took a step closer to her.

Her eyes widened. A pulse thrummed visibly in a small vein in her neck.

"Me neither." She couldn't scramble inside her little car fast enough. "My quest for adventure ended Saturday night."

Damn. He'd advanced too quickly. He was still operating as if Mia was really the wild child he'd met Saturday at Gasparilla, when all signs were pointing to her being much more complicated than that.

This called for a carefully laid plan.

"I want to see you again, Mia." He'd never chased down any woman like this, had never needed to work so hard for a date. But some gut instinct pushed him forward, urged him to explore whatever it was that had combusted between them. "We can find adventure that will make Saturday look like kid's play."

She punched a control on her dashboard while she slammed the door shut. Luckily, the top to her convertible folded back on itself in response, exposing her to his gaze again, bathing her in the warm sunshine of the day.

He should have known she'd appreciate the hairblowing, wind-in-your-face ride of a ragtop. She'd taken such obvious delight in tearing through the waves on his boat the other night. She hadn't cared that she'd ended up dripping wet or that she'd ruined her flower. Perhaps being an artist gave her a deeper appreciation for any experience that indulged the senses.

That notion gave immediate…rise…to his own senses. If the woman delighted in simple pleasures like wind through her hair or the salty spray of ocean water over her body, how much might she enjoy more carnal pursuits?

"I can't see you anymore, Seth." She turned the key in the ignition and started the motor. "But I had fun on our adventure—kid's play or not." The smile she gave him stole the breath he was going to take right out of his mouth. "Thanks for a wild ride."

By the time his breathing kicked in again, he stood staring at taillights and her retreating license plate, which clearly read "Pinellas County" along the bottom.

She might not be in the phonebook, but she couldn't live too far away if her car was registered within the county.

Her siren's voice ringing in his ears, Seth determined their wild ride would definitely not be their last. He'd never allowed himself to be beaten before, and Mia's refusal had just presented him with a challenge too irresistible to ignore. Deep down, she still wanted adventure, right?

He would make it his business to be certain he was the man to deliver her every last exotic fantasy in order to win her back.

"HEY HONEY, want to go for a ride?" Noelle Quentin arrived home at the same time as Mia, only instead of driving her usual car, Mia's mother now sat on a shiny black moped, a scratched helmet with a peeling Bonnie Raitt decal strapped to her head.

With her shoulder length dark hair and average height, Noelle resembled her daughter in many ways. Only Mia's golden skin gave away her Latin heritage from her father.

Noelle didn't look a day over twenty-five even though she was fast approaching her fortieth birthday. Something about her perpetual teasing smile and the energetic way she charged through life caused people to regularly mistake her for Mia's sister.

Mia shut the door to her convertible and tugged her weekend bag out of the back seat. She'd been in the driveway for approximately twenty seconds and already trouble was brewing.

"Not right now, Mom. Where'd you get the moped?"

Noelle could definitely afford a motorbike, but she'd been assuring the family she would use every dime from her teaching job at a community college to put toward a bonafide house. She'd been living in a hotel suite for the past three years—just one more way she seemed to communicate her presence in Twin Palms was temporary.

Again.

"I'm borrowing this from a bike shop up the coast to see if I want one of my own." She flipped her shoulder length brown hair over one shoulder and smiled. "Can't you see me cruising onto campus with this everyday?"

"Max speed on that is what, ten miles an hour? You could probably run there faster."

"And arrive sweaty?" Noelle pouted, drawing an ever-present dimple in her cheek downward along with her perfectly painted rose-colored mouth. "I don't think so. I may be losing my looks, but I'm definitely keeping my vanity. Besides, think how much money I'll save if I trade in my car for one of these."

Mia nearly dropped her bag. How many times would her mother ride headlong into disaster?

"You're not seriously thinking of trading in the Honda for a moped."

Noelle shrugged as she unstrapped the helmet. "I'm trying to liquidate some assets anyway, and I thought you might need a financial boost with the store—"

So that's what this was about. "No. Not a good idea. What if you need to take Gramp to the doctor when I'm not here? Or what if it rains? If the Beachcomber is going to succeed, it's got to be self sufficient and not just eat up money we pour into it from outside resources."

Noelle turned to stare at the charming storefront that had been her parents' dream. Mia looked too, struggling to see the place objectively. She'd lived over the store with her grandparents until she went away to college. Now she kept her own place in a converted boathouse behind the marina, but Mia still viewed the store and the apartment above it as home.

The weathered cedar shingles had worn well, but the sign out front was faded and dated, the display windows old-fashioned and still cracked from the last hurricane season.

"The Beachcomber isn't ever going to be an independent business unless you take drastic measures to modernize it inside and out. The merchandise is as antiquated as everything else about it, Mia, whether you allow yourself to admit that or not." Noelle took the weight of Mia's small suitcase onto her own shoulder while Mia carried in her purse and papers. "I know you don't want to hurt your grandparents' feelings, but they need to hear it from someone. Someone who's not me, that is. How was your trip?''

Exciting because she'd had a close encounter with a gorgeous man. Disappointing because she hadn't seen him naked. Scary because she feared she wouldn't forget Seth any time soon.

Of course, who shared that with their mother?

''It was okay,'' Mia hedged, unwilling to reveal so much as a whisper about Seth even if he had turned her world upside down. ''The bank is at least giving me a few more weeks to pull a rabbit out of my hat before they foreclose.''

Noelle dropped the overnight bag. It fell with a thunk on the wooden steps up to the shop's back entrance. ''It's really come down to that?''

Mia paused on the steps so as not to step on her bag full of fun weekend clothes, though God knew, she wouldn't be needing anything sultry and sexy for a long time now that she had a miracle to pull off in the form of slave labor.

''Don't worry. I'm hoping this will give me the impetus to forge ahead with updating the place without feeling guilty that I'm altering something Grammie and Gramp worked so hard to create. I've been slowly collecting new inventory for years.''

Nodding fast and frequently, as if she could somehow convince herself all would be well, Noelle reached to retrieve her daughter's bag. ''That's a great plan if it works. And it would all be worth it if you can put the kibosh on those 'My mom and dad went to Florida and all I got was this stupid shirt' holdovers from fifteen years ago. You know *I'm* behind you one hundred percent.''

''You don't think Grammie and Gramp will be though, do you?''

''I think they will come around when they realize how serious the financial concerns are. You've been protecting them from too much, Mia, and it's time they knew these renovations are a last-ditch, make-or-break effort.'' She opened the door to let them into the store. ''Now please tell me you had some serious fun this weekend to tide you over for the next few weeks of hell?''

Of course Noelle was more interested in girl talk than business. From all appearances, the woman had never been crazy about motherhood or anything so boring as responsibilities.

Before Mia could dodge the question, they ran into Frankie Bollino, manager of the marina next door and Mia's landlord, as he exited the Beachcomber.

''Did I hear you say something about Mia and fun? I think she forgot how to make the two go together, Noelle.'' He winked at Mia to mitigate his words. ''That is, unless she's harboring an inner wild child she's not telling us about?''

Mia backed into the store's shaky wooden porch railing. Frankie had always been more than a little interested in her inner wild child. Her grandparents had been fooled into thinking he was a great guy because he was local—for them, the real test of a suitable bachelor lay in his ability to stay close to home.

Grammie and Gramp weren't much for adventure. At least not for their offspring.

"Not a chance," Mia replied. "I spent my spare time working on my income tax forms and transferring some old phone numbers into a new address book."

Frankie rolled his eyes and edged past them. "Want me to take your suitcase to the boathouse for you? I can leave it on the porch."

Okay, so maybe he wasn't such a bad guy. "Thanks. If you're sure you don't mind."

He had the bag on one arm and was halfway down the stairs before she had the words out her mouth.

"No problem," he called over his shoulder as he ducked between two palm trees that stood sentinel in front of the boathouse.

"Frankie really is cute," her mother assured her as they edged into the store.

He was also really *not* Seth. For some reason, Mia could only think about a certain two-faced banking tycoon with pockets as big as the holes in hers. Not that she could afford to figure things out with Seth right now anyway. Work would command her world for the next few weeks. After that, she needed to find some way to reclaim her own life, and her art. She didn't need a gorgeous man confusing her about what she really wanted out of life.

She had family to do that for her, thank you very much.

Spying her grandmother and grandfather bent over a display model shuffleboard game, Mia took a deep breath and wished she didn't have to upset them today. Her grandparents had sacrificed so much of their time and limited financial resources to raise Mia, to send her to the best schools. She prayed they would understand why she needed to make changes to their beloved store. She only wanted to give them the secure retirement they deserved.

Too bad she'd have to wage a family civil war to do so.

Shoving all lingering thoughts of pirates and naked men aside, she launched in with both guns loaded.

"According to the bank, we've got a few weeks before foreclosure proceedings begin. But the loan officer assured me if we could somehow drag the Beachcomber into the new millennium and show some earning potential before then they might be persuaded to put that off—"

"Mia Teresa Quentin shame on you." Betty Quentin straightened from her shuffleboard game, her stick tapping out an impatient time against her foot. She looked every one of her seventy-plus years with her marked wrinkles and faded silver hair, but her proud bearing, her purple running suit and the crimson T-shirt underneath it proclaimed her sense of pride in her age. "My phone has been ringing off the hook with gossip about you on television at the Gasparilla festival in the arms of some bare-chested buccaneer."

Oh no. And Mia thought *she* was walking into this family meeting with her guns loaded? Grammie had just leveled her with a well-aimed torpedo.

Noelle cut her eyes toward Mia, a wicked grin on

her face. "Yes, *do* tell. Did you manage to have some fun in spite of all Grandma's warnings?"

"Noelle, please. We are only worried about Mia." Betty dropped her stick into her husband's lap and crossed the store to put a comforting arm around Mia's neck. "I'm sure it was some sort of publicity stunt you agreed to do to promote the festival?"

Noelle sighed. "Please say no. I couldn't bear to hear you'd been that close to having fun and that you hadn't indulged."

"That damn festival is probably a chamber of commerce special—all commercial glitz and no heart," Norman Quentin grumbled from his seat beside the shuffleboard. "Too damn bad we didn't have something like that in Twin Palms for the Beachcomber to benefit from. You can bet we'd be selling some pink flamingo lawn ornaments then."

Mia didn't dare glance in her mother's direction after *that* comment. "Actually, Grammie, I volunteered to be a part of the Gasparilla festival because I thought it looked like harmless fun, and—"

Grammie's face contorted into an incensed pucker, almost as if she'd swallowed a lemon. "Being carried off in your sarong by a muscle-bound dunderhead privateer who probably surfs for a living is fun?"

"—and I felt like I deserved some fun after the long hours I've been putting in at the store lately." Mia adored her grandmother, but it was important to finish your sentences in these conversations or Grammie would steamroll right over you. "And he wasn't a dunderhead."

"But was he muscle-bound?" Noelle asked, waggling her eyebrows and no doubt adding fuel to the grandparent fire.

Mia ground her teeth together and smiled—a combination she'd long ago perfected during family time. For as long as she could remember, Noelle had been carefully pushing her parents' buttons, but Mia had never fully understood why.

Perhaps some of it was a holdover from the long-ago subtle custody battles over who should raise Mia, but that didn't seem to fully account for it.

"I hardly noticed if he had muscles, mother, I was too busy—"

"Memorizing the tax table?" Noelle supplied.

"—thinking about how to save the Beachcomber from financial ruin." Maybe she was using unfair tactics here, but *someone* had to consider the real-life ramifications of her trip to Tampa. The pirate fantasy had definitely crashed and burned when Seth refused her advances. It flat-out disintegrated when she'd realized he'd lied to her.

"The fact is, we've got two weeks to work our tails off to attract some business and make some improvements here before the bank forecloses," Mia explained, fingering a wind-up alligator sitting on the front counter. "Apparently, bankers are quick to foreclose on property like this because the real estate is so valuable. But if we can update the store a bit and attract some new business we might be able to at least show some good faith on our end. They might float the loan a few more months while we get back on our feet.'' And overhaul everything the elder Quentins loved about their little shop.

Her grandparents frowned in unison, but Norman spoke first. ''Update the Beachcomber?''

Mia prepared for Round Two. Now that she'd successfully shuffled the focus from Seth to the store, she still had to convince them to make changes in the shop—something she hadn't been able to do her whole life. But right now, failing wasn't an option.

She would never be free to pursue her dream of painting full-time if she didn't find a way to make her grandparents' business self-sufficient. If ever there had been a time to be aggressive, this was it.

Fortunately, her adventure with Seth had taught her she *could* be aggressive. She only needed to clear her mind of the sexy thoughts that had plagued her ever since she left him standing in the bank parking lot, focus on the business at hand and think about the ultimate goal—her art.

Too bad her vision of the ultimate goal kept getting mixed up with an X-rated image of Seth.

Since when had she become so man-crazy? If she wasn't careful, she'd be buying a moped and tooling back to Tampa to jump Seth after all. Mia loved her mom, but she had no intention of leading her life with the same abandon Noelle always had.

''Yes, update the Beachcomber,'' Mia finally responded, shaking off her muddled thoughts. ''There are going to be some big changes around here....''

Not the least of which was going to be that Mia was never thinking about Seth Chandler or orgasmic kisses again.

SETH TURNED the dial on the eyepiece of his binoculars and watched the letters of the dilapidated sign come into focus—Beachcomber.

"That's it," he called to his uncle over the dull roar of the boat engines. "The gray cedar building right next to the marina."

Seth had the address thanks to Brock's access to the police computer. Seth could have checked in Mia's bank record, but that didn't seem right to him. All he wanted was her address, not her financial history.

Because he only wanted Brock to unearth the basic information, his uncle assured him he wasn't being too unethical. Nevertheless, the stubborn former cop had decided he ought to be present when Seth went to see Mia.

Now Brock eased up on the engine as he veered toward the shore. "I'll check out the bait at the marina while you woo your woman. If she doesn't boot you out on your butt by the time I'm done, I'll just be fishing until you're ready to head back to town."

"You really didn't need to come out here with me."

"I've seen how you treat your boat. No way was I going to loan *Betsy* to you." Brock edged the boat toward the marina's pier. "Besides, what if you need some advice on how to handle the whole Mia thing?"

"Like I'm going to ask you, a crusty bachelor who probably hasn't dated since the eighties?" Seth tossed a rope around an iron hook on the dock and pulled it taut.

"I'm just waiting on the right woman. Fishermen know the value of patience."

"Great. Read the finer points of relationships in Brock Chandler's *Zen Fishing and the Art of Dating*. Sounds like a bestseller." Seth vaulted out of the boat, hauling a bouquet the size of a small tree along with him.

Brock stepped out behind him, just in time to tweak a hibiscus in Seth's arms. "Most women prefer substance over style, college boy. But good luck."

Damn. As they walked up the dock together, Seth assured himself Brock was just trying to screw with his mind. The flower offering seemed perfectly appropriate, especially when he remembered how much sensual pleasure Mia had derived from toying with the petals of the hibiscus on his boat.

Following his instincts had paid off in a big way when it came to the stock market. But he couldn't rule out the possibility that his instincts sucked when it came to relationships—Brock had a point there.

Nevertheless, he needed an excuse to walk back into Mia's life and the flowers in his arms gave him just that. He'd give Mia flowers now—adventure later.

They reached the end of the dock and were about to split ways when a commotion emanating from the Beachcomber reached their ears.

A man shouting. Multiple women shouting.

Followed by a loud crash.

Seth and Brock sprinted toward the tourist shop, scaling the narrow steps, and crashing their way through the entrance. The stood in the door, ready to take on robbers, muggers or other villains, but found only an old man and woman wailing holy hell at Mia and another dark-haired woman, most certainly her sister.

They all stood frozen in a semicircle, gazing down at the sea of fallen pink flamingo lawn ornaments around their feet. A shelf above their heads still swung on one nail like a pendulum against the back wall.

"Need some help?" Seth offered from the doorway, unsure how to rectify the absurd scene that had obviously distressed the elderly couple. Mia's grandparents, perhaps? The older man looked ready to cry while the silver-haired woman dressed in a purple running suit was clearly ready to strangle Mia and her sister.

His words seemed to break the moment. In the back of his mind, Seth noticed the wailing ceased, but he couldn't be bothered to confirm the fact. His brain was far too occupied absorbing every inch of Mia Quentin.

Her straight, dark hair no longer draped her body in a sensual curtain. Now, it twisted around itself in a long braid that disappeared behind her back. She wore faded jean shorts that accented her slender, tanned legs and a yellow Miami Hurricanes sweatshirt with the sleeves rolled up. Barely-there wire-rimmed glasses perched on her nose.

He'd never seen a woman be so sexy without even trying. She'd looked phenomenal when he met her last weekend, yet these frayed denim shorts made the sarong look like sackcloth. No two ways about it, Mia Quentin was hot.

Thankfully, the older woman marched forward, regaining composure before anyone else in the room and effectively snapping him out of ogling-mode.

"Help? Of course not. Why don't you gentlemen come on in and look around?" The woman's smile was automatic, but not entirely without warmth. She had a lifetime in small-town retail written all over her. "I would be happy to help *you*. We're technically closed this week for repairs, but we never turn away customers."

Seth waited for Brock to say something. Shouldn't Brock be running interference for him so he could go stare at—no, talk to—Mia?

A glance in his uncle's direction found the confirmed bachelor's eyes roving Mia's older sister with undisguised interest, however.

So much for help from that quarter.

"No thanks." Seth produced the bouquet that had lost a few petals in his haste to save Mia from the commotion a few minutes ago. "Actually, I came to see Mia."

The older woman stopped her forward progress. The old man issued a distinct harrumph. No doubt, this had to be the grandfather who grew an ulcer for every guy Mia dated.

Mia jumped into action at her grandfather's distress. She patted the man's shoulder soothingly before stepping over the pile of wooden flamingos. "Maybe now isn't the best time—"

The woman who looked like Mia's sister leaped

into the discussion. "Now is a great time! Mia, go chat with your guest and I'll figure out what to do with all these pink birds." She threw an arm around Mia's shoulders and anchored her a few feet in front of Seth. "Maybe we'll have a bonfire on the beach and invite the neighbors."

"Mom," Mia sighed between her teeth and delivered an elbow into the other woman's side. Grandma and Grandpa grumbled in the background.

"You're her mother?" Brock the Bachelor stepped forward, the surly fisherman facade momentarily dropped in favor of suave gentleman caller. He flashed more teeth than Seth could remember seeing in fifteen years. "You don't look nearly old enough to be her mother."

"She's not," Grandma groused from behind them, her helpful shop clerk manner long vanished. "Didn't I tell you boys we were closed today?"

Mia and her mother exchanged a glance Seth couldn't quite interpret but which no doubt had something to do with family commiseration over grouchy predecessors.

"Why don't we step outside," Mia suggested, more subtly diplomatic than her mother. "Grammie, you and Grandpa relax and I'll stack up the birds in a few minutes."

A few minutes? That's all he warranted in the aftermath of the most scorching kisses of his life?

If he had anything to say about it, he was turning those few minutes into a few hours. Too bad Brock and Mia's mother stuck to them like barnacles as they headed out the store and down the steps toward the pier.

"You can go buy your bait now, Brock," Seth reminded his uncle loudly. "I bet the marina next door will have something."

"They have everything," Mia's mother confirmed as she moved away from the group, seemingly unmoved by Brock's new savoir faire. "I'll just take a ride on the moped and get out of your hair while you two...talk." Her wink let Seth know he'd found an ally.

As she backed away toward the motorbike in the driveway, Brock scowled at Seth.

"Don't you know you never discuss bait while romancing a woman?" Brock jogged toward the motorbike and the woman who'd obviously caught his eye. Over one shoulder he called, "Watch and learn, Romeo."

Leaving Seth alone with Mia. Finally.

Now he could go launch a damage-repair mission and get things back on track with her.

"Sorry to interrupt whatever you were doing in there," Seth started, holding the bouquet of flowers in front of him like a shield. "I came out here to give you these."

He spied a hint of longing in her eyes as she hovered over the bouquet, inhaling the fragrant blooms. She reached to touch a petal before she jerked back.

"They're gorgeous, but—"

"Or to invite you to dinner. Or to an art show. Or for a weekend in Paris. You name it." All he needed was one date to give her the adventure she craved—

one chance to uncover the sensualist he'd glimpsed over the weekend. He set the flowers down on a bench built into the dock.

"You can't be serious." Her hands clenched and unclenched over the bouquet, giving Seth a few ideas about how to lure this sensual woman.

"I'm very serious."

"Hasn't anyone ever told you no before, Chandler?" She blew a strand of dark hair out of her eye.

Seth told himself he'd be pushing his luck if he were to smooth that silky lock with his fingers, but it was all he could do not to touch her.

"People tell me 'no' all the time in my business."

"Do you ever listen?"

"Not when it's this important."

She shook her head, her dark eyebrows knit in confusion. "What's so important, Seth? A thwarted weekend fling? Let's face it, we didn't share all that much."

"That's because I'm not the kind of guy to ravish-and-run. I wanted to get to know you."

Some of the exasperation fled her features, to be replaced by something less wary, more curious. She swayed forward ever so slightly. "You're here because you want to get to know me?"

Seth allowed himself to lean in another fraction of an inch, careful not to scare her off, but ready to capitalize on some of the spark that leaped every time they came within touching distance.

"I want to know you so badly I couldn't wait for my boat to get fixed next week. I let my uncle drive me out here because I needed to see you, needed to know where you'd disappeared to the other day.'' He canted closer, their breath mingling in the already hot air between them.

The quick pulse at her throat gave him all the invitation he needed to press his suit.

This time, he was laying his cards on the table.

''I want to know you in the friendly sense, the biblical sense and the carnal sense, Mia, and I'm not leaving until you tell me when I can see you again.''

7

NOELLE WAS TWO FEET from her moped escape route when the linebacker disguised as a longshoreman caught up with her. Who *was* this guy stomping around Twin Palms in fishing boots, worn-out Levi's and shoulders the size of Texas anyway?

Despite the hot looks he'd been tossing her way ever since he burst in the door with Mia's pirate, he was definitely not her type. Way too dangerous looking with that unshaven jaw, close-cropped dark hair and a scar the size of her pinkie running down one cheek. These days, she preferred her men tame and trainable.

Besides, even if she'd had the inclination to flirt, she definitely didn't have the time—not with such an important appointment waiting for her just up the street.

"Mind if I ride along?" he asked, slowing to a stop next to her even though she knew he had to have run his very nice-looking butt off to have reached her already.

"A ride?" It took her a minute to figure out what he was talking about. Something about the warmth in his dark gaze distracted her just a little. "On the moped?"

Shrugging, he flashed her a crooked smile and pointed behind him with a jerk of his thumb. "Looks like your daughter is going to be visiting with my nephew for a while and I hate to be stuck hanging around all by myself during the soap opera to follow."

His voice rasped through the warm summer air like a younger Bruce Springsteen—just rough enough to inspire vaguely sordid thoughts.

Noelle squinted past him to see Mia and her pirate talking, their body language communicating an encouraging intensity. She would be very glad to see her daughter get caught up in her own personal soap opera for a change.

"Actually, I'm late for…an appointment." It wasn't a lie, even though it made the perfect excuse for a woman intent on ignoring the longshoreman's obvious overtures.

Noelle didn't have too many talents to her credit, but easing her way out of relationships with men and avoiding commitment at all costs ranked as a specialty she prided herself on.

Unfortunately, her latest pursuer couldn't seem to take a hint. He reached for one of the helmets perched on the seat.

"Then why don't you let me drive you and save you some time." His hand hovered between the two helmets—the plain spare one, and hers with the women of rock and roll decals plastered all over it. "Who gets Bonnie Raitt?"

"Not you." Noelle snatched up her helmet, unable to reconcile the image of this burly fisherman wearing girlie protective gear. "You'd look ridiculous in a moped helmet and I'm not driving to my appointment anyway."

So much for the moped escape. But she would not share that tiny seat with her oversize companion.

She would walk, but she was afraid if she said that, he'd be two steps behind her. And she wanted—needed—privacy for this mission.

"Look, why don't you go back into the store?" she offered, not wanting to be rude to a friend of Mia's pirate but starting to worry she'd miss her appointment all together. "My mother always appreciates company."

"Your mother?" The man looked confused for all of a second before a smile caught at his lips and spread across his stern features. "I've got a better idea. How about I go back into the store and have a chat with your mother about your clandestine appointment?"

Her jaw probably landed somewhere around the moped seat. How could this guy possibly know her meeting was a secret?

"I'm Brock Chandler, by the way." He reached across the moped to extend her his hand. "You sure I can't go with you?"

Noelle folded her arms across her chest, vaguely aware her feminine curiosity had been piqued very much against her will. "Are you trying to blackmail me into accepting your company?"

"I'm just trying to avoid another go-round with the pink flamingoes." Brock withdrew his outstretched hand. "What do you say?"

"Fine. But you can't ask any questions or get in the way. And we can walk because it's actually just around the corner." Sighing, she started down the sidewalk past the marina, amazed she'd allowed him to coerce her into doing something she hadn't really wanted to. Had any man accomplished that feat since the night she'd gotten pregnant with Mia?

Probably not.

And oddly, she had the feeling maybe she didn't mind the longshoreman's company all that much anyway. There was a peculiar comfort in listening to those soft-soled boots pad down the sidewalk behind her as she approached the biggest appointment of her life.

"Can I at least ask your name?"

Men pushing forty weren't nearly as trainable as those pushing thirty.

"Noelle Quentin, and all bets are off if you ask me anything else." She was snippy when she was nervous and damn it all, she was nervous now as she looked up at the small antique store that had closed shop last summer.

She had no business being here. No right to dream her own selfish dreams when Mia wasn't being given the opportunity to live hers. What right did Noelle have to her own business, to a small stake in happiness, when her daughter currently shouldered enough responsibilities for three generations?

It had been a mistake to come look at this building.

She would have run back to the Beachcomber if it hadn't been for the massive obstacle of man standing a scant foot behind her.

Curious, she half turned to check for other routes of escape. But Brock's dark eyes studied her far too closely, missing nothing. The heat of his body suddenly seemed to surround her, reminding her of the sorts of intimacies she hadn't shared in much too long.

"Leaving so soon?"

His words broke the seductive pull of his warmth.

"That counts as a question, buster. You're out of here." She pointed a finger in his face for good measure, needing to assure herself she was feeling righteous indignation and not a major attack of hormones.

Unfortunately, she couldn't enforce Brock's exit just then because her Realtor finally appeared.

Then Brock turned up the charm another notch, following the Realtor and Noelle from room to room in the empty antique shop. The fraud even went so far as to pretend an interest in Noelle's most secret wish—a dream the Realtor unwittingly revealed as the young woman pointed out features of the building that would lend themselves to a coffeehouse complete with moped rental facilities.

An hour later, Noelle found herself back on the street with Brock after parting with the Realtor.

Even after the young woman drove out of sight, Brock continued to peruse the spec sheets they'd been given on the property. As if he gave a flying fish hook about her dream business locale.

"Moped rentals?"

Noelle squeezed the bridge of her nose, wishing the fisherman smelled more like fish and less like

laundry detergent and ocean breezes. "I can't believe
you would continue to ask intrusive questions when
you have so overstayed your welcome. Haven't you
got anything better to do than hound a defenseless
woman?"

He grinned with no remorse, crinkling that scar of
his right in half with a narrow dimple. "That's not
hounding, Noelle, that's called having patience with
you. And I'd hardly call you defenseless, as I'm sure
you well know." He handed over his copy of the
spec sheet to her. "More like an armored fortress."

Noelle seized on his words, ruthlessly shutting out
the enticing memory of his dimple. She would not
allow herself to get distracted by a man again. Ever.

"That's right, buster. A heavily armed fortress that
hasn't allowed anyone through the gates in a good
many years. You'd be better served taking your patience and your charm and spending it on another,
less well-defended woman."

For some reason, her words—delivered with
plenty of sass and even a little finger pointing—failed
to make him back up so much as a step. In fact, the
linebacker loomed a bit closer.

"I'd never launch an assault on such a heavily
guarded stronghold, Noelle."

Her heart jumped in a quirky tune at that news.
Damned foolish organ. Still, something about the
heat in his gaze, the wide stance of his jean-encased
thighs, made her mildly...curious. Surprisingly flustered.

"You wouldn't?" Her voice cracked just a little,

her repartee inexcusably dull for a woman who'd practically seen it all in her wild lifetime.

"No." He moved in closer, bringing their bodies within inches of one another, cranking up her temperature a few more degrees. "The best offense in this case is to call out the opponent from their hiding place."

"So you can find all their weaknesses?" She'd definitely seen that maneuver before and she'd be damned if she'd stick around for it again. Not waiting for an answer, she pivoted on her heel.

His fingers slipped around her wrist before she could go, gently encircling her arm.

Heat pumped through her at that feathery caress. She could push away from him easily, but somehow Brock's light touch made her wish she could stay.

"No." That gravelly Springsteen voice tripped down her spine, tingling every available nerve on its way. "So I can start negotiating for a little peace and harmony."

Noelle couldn't help but smile at that image. "A scarred longshoreman in fishing boots hardly seems like an effective diplomat."

He trailed his light touch up one arm to curve over her shoulder.

Awareness turned her skin to gooseflesh, called her nipples to tight attention beneath her blouse.

"That's where you're wrong, Noelle. Diplomacy isn't necessarily achieved with an olive branch." One thumb stroked the length of her exposed collarbone.

She gulped for air, wished for another brush of that thumb. "No?"

"Sometimes the best way to achieve peace is by more underhanded means."

"Such as?"

His mouth grazed hers. Her eyelids fluttered closed for a fraction of a second before she forced them back open.

"How about sexual blackmail?"

She blinked. The liquid rush of heat through her veins didn't slow for a second, however. "Excuse me?"

His steady gaze held hers.

"Blackmail, Noelle. As in you forfeit a seriously hot kiss right now or I broadcast the moped plan to the whole damn world."

MIA BLINKED, waiting for her brain to unscramble the message Seth Chandler had just delivered.

Surely the man who'd been so noble in the face of her killer red lace bathing suit hadn't just said he wanted to know her in the carnal sense?

She was so caught off guard that she didn't protest when he pulled her away from her grandparents' shop and out onto the stretch of public beach in front of it. White sand stretched for miles in a narrow strip up the coast. Even in February, they had to navigate around beach towels and little tents erected for shade.

Their steps slowed as they reached a wooden bench at the foot of a bridge spanning sand dunes, sea oats and beach grasses. Seth pulled her to sit beside him.

''I want you, Mia. Badly.'' His brown eyes locked on hers, dark, intense—hot.

She didn't realize she was already shaking her head, silently denying him, until Seth's fingers cupped her chin to stop the motion.

''Don't say no.''

His thumb smoothed over her bottom lip, a remarkably sensual gesture that sent a shiver over her skin.

''I don't have time in my life right now.'' Besides, when a man could make her feel as weak-willed and warm-blooded as Seth could, she worried she was as susceptible to men as her mother always had been.

His fingers edged back down her throat and behind her hair to curve around the base of her neck. His khaki-covered thigh grazed against her bare leg.

''Shouldn't there always be time for pleasure?'' His slow, deliberate pronunciation of the last word tripped through her like a caress.

''I've got a lot to accomplish.'' It sounded like a flimsy argument even to her own ears. But she couldn't seem to make her brain focus on her burning need to establish herself as an artist.

In fact, she could only seem to concentrate on one burning need right how, and it was all because of Seth's nearness.

''I could help you.'' His voice whispered across her temple.

And made her remember precisely why she wasn't going to get caught up with a man for anything more than a sordid one-night stand.

''I definitely don't need help.'' Her mother and

grandparents had been arguing over who could help her more from the day she was born. The last thing she wanted was to add a helpful man to the mix. "Besides, men seem to have a great capacity to promise help and not deliver."

Noelle had gone through enough men who'd lied to get her into bed that she could probably start her own football team.

Okay, maybe only a basketball team. But still—

Mia had learned from her mother's mistakes.

Seth's fingers continued to toy with the hair at her nape, sending spirals of tingling sensation through her shoulders and down her back.

"I'm not like that, Mia."

Something in his dark gaze made her want to believe him, and that was dangerous, scary territory.

She was seeing a new side of Seth today. Bold Seth. Intent-as-hell Seth. The driven determination that had no doubt helped make him a corporate tycoon at a young age.

That fierce ambition might work in the boardroom, but it wouldn't work with her.

"It doesn't matter," she assured him, tugging his hands out of her hair. "I can't go to an art show, and I can't go to Paris. I can't be with you, Seth, not the way you'd like me to be."

She waited for him to give up and go home. Oddly, he continued to sit across from her, assessing her with his too-clever gaze.

"What about adventure?"

His remark found its target, cutting into the fine

threads of her hopes and dreams. Seth Chandler understood her secret wish better than anyone.

"I will find it without you." Although "adventure" with any other man didn't hold near the appeal after glimpsing the kind of effect Seth could have on her.

She hadn't forgotten the earth-moving orgasm he'd given her with no more than a kiss. And heaven help her, she wanted another one of those orgasms before she sent him packing.

"When?"

"Some day." She shifted in her seat. "Soon."

Seth watched Mia's restless movements, knowing she was lying through her teeth. She'd probably never sought adventure in her whole life until she'd jumped into his arms screaming at the Gasparilla festival.

To a certain extent, she'd *chosen* him to rescue her that day, hadn't she? Mia had leaped into his arms, hoping he'd provide her with the excitement that had been missing from her life.

Now the time had come for him to prove he could provide all the thrills she could handle.

"Fine." He nodded agreement, thankful ten years of business training had taught him how to bluff with the best. "If you're really too busy to explore things between us, then I'm out of here."

Surprise fluttered across her features, and was it wishful thinking, or did a hint of disappointment pinch the corners of those full, gorgeous lips?

"Thanks for understanding—"

"Just as soon as I get one last kiss."

Her mouth opened, but no sound came out. For a moment, Seth toyed with the idea of moving in for a kiss right then and there, but he really wanted her to accept his proposition first.

"A kiss?" She fidgeted with the tail of her braid, winding her finger around and around the length of rawhide she'd used to tie it all together.

"One kiss and I'm out of here." Hopefully with her whole-hearted agreement they needed to see one another again. And again. He flashed her his best I'm-a-harmless-guy grin, unwilling to let her see how much was riding on her consent. "You game?"

Once her head tilted to the side, as if she silently weighed any potential consequences, Seth knew he'd won. Still, he waited for the actual words to leave her lips.

Finally, she smiled.

"Okay." Her green cat eyes alit with the latent mischief he hadn't seen since she'd stripped off her sarong to tease him that night on the boat. "What harm could there be in one kiss?"

Before she could ponder that particular question too thoroughly, Seth wasted no time moving in. He allotted one hand to each of her shoulders and pulled her closer, slanted his mouth over hers and kissed the lips that had been so prominent in his fantasies for the past three days.

She tasted like sea breezes and herbal tea. Salty and sweet and perfect.

Just like on the boat, she didn't hold anything back. He'd never met a woman who kissed like Mia Quentin, and he definitely had way too many experiences to compare it to. Maybe she'd never learned to be coy, had never found it necessary to develop degrees of kissing—a "thanks, it's been fun" kiss, the "reserved exploration" kiss, or the "let's step this up a notch" kiss.

No, Mia offered everything with one press of her delicate, sensitive lips. From the way she broke all boundaries of personal space to get as close to him as possible, to the way she closed her eyes as if to tune into her sense of touch all the more, Mia took everything she could from a kiss, and man, did she ever give it all back.

Her breath quickened when he smoothed his hands down her arms and onto her waist. Her heart picked up the pace as he pulled her body fully against his, breasts to chest.

She felt so good against him, so sweetly right, he found himself forgetting all about his well-planned objectives. What had he been going to wrest from her with this sizzling meeting of mouths?

More than a little affected himself, Seth ignored the annoying voice in the back of his brain and pulled her right into his lap. She made a high-pitched sound that was half squeal and half moan as her thigh skimmed against the rock solid length of him barely contained by his khakis.

Damn, but he was letting himself enjoy this far too much. If he didn't get his head together soon, this great kiss would be wasted. She'd come to her senses before he remembered what the hell he was supposed to be talking her into right now.

Before he could regroup, however, a long, low

wolf whistle reminded them of their public display. A group of bikini-clad beach bunnies walked by just as Mia and Seth broke apart, pointing and giggling.

Mia pulled away from him by a fraction, her breath fanning his cheek with soft pants. "Maybe you should come back tonight," she whispered, then kissed him again. "Just for a little while."

Oh yeah.

If Seth had been capable of shouting with victory, he might have, but right now, all he could think about was driving Mia insane, making her want him as much as he wanted her.

He trailed one hand up her side to graze the curve of her breast and she trembled in his arms.

"Later," she urged, pushing him away with her hands even though she continued to kiss him, continued to light his fire with every swirl of her salty-sweet tongue. "Meet me at my house."

"Let's go there now." Had he honestly said that? Where the hell was his restraint? His poker face? His freaking legendary ability to negotiate for better position?

"We can't." Mia wriggled off his lap and pulled her mouth from his.

Her green eyes blinked open to meet his gaze, full of heat and a promise that made him want to lay her on the bench right then and there and—

"I've got a lot of work to do this afternoon, but we can continue this…discussion…later." Her voice drifted on the breeze with husky overtones, the sexy drawl of a woman ready to play.

"I'll be there." His own voice sounded like he was hung over and hoarse to boot.

God, this woman did a number on him.

Before he could pull out any smooth lines about what he was going to do to her tonight, she jogged down the beach away from him. Her tanned legs flexed taut muscles against the frayed denim of her shorts, her simple yellow sweatshirt putting Bo Derek and all her braids to shame.

He ran a hand over his eyes and down his face in a lame attempt to get a grip again. The woman damn near turned him inside out with her no-holds-barred approach to sexuality.

Damn, he could hardly wait for tonight.

8

RAMPANT CASE of lust—one.

Rational thinking—zip.

Okay, so maybe her decision to invite Seth over tonight had been rash and reckless and dangerously akin to a vintage Noelle move, Mia thought as she slapped more white paint on her canvas to cover up the big, fat mistake she just made.

One of many today, it seemed.

At least she could fix the yellow tail she'd accidentally given the Big Bad Wolf in her new fairy-tale collage. She had no clue how to fix what had happened with Seth today. He'd be here sometime tonight because she couldn't seem to pick up the phone and tell him she'd changed her mind.

She wanted him as much as ever. More by the hour, even. Although Mia had played it safe with men the few and far between times she'd had an opportunity to date, Seth Chandler shot down every cautious instinct she possessed. She was a wild woman around him and she couldn't seem to help herself. A situation that needed to be rectified sooner or later, but just now, Mia leaned toward later. Maybe a night with Seth would take the edge off her need for him, satisfy the constant craving that had developed ever since he swung down from the deck of the *Jose Gaspar* and into her life.

Besides, his peculiar effect on her—making her feel daring and ready to take a risk—had prompted her to call an art dealer in Tampa who'd been asking her for months to let him organize a gallery showing. Mia needed the money a big show could net, and her afternoon with Seth had given her a boost in confidence.

Or foolishness. Either way, she needed to start preparing for a show next week. If she was going to start experiencing life more fully, she deserved a night with Seth for herself.

Mia squinted at her canvas critically. The Big Bad Wolf had looked much safer with a yellow tail, but she had never been the kind of artist to sugarcoat the truth. The Three Little Pigs would just have to reckon with the tall, dark and dangerous version—the wolf in Italian loafers.

The doorbell rang, causing her brush to jump right out of her hand.

"Mia?" Noelle pushed open the front door without waiting for an invitation. "Can I come in?"

Great. Now her mother was bound to catch her in the one rash act of a lifetime.

"Actually, I'm expecting company soon." She bent to pick up her brush then walked straight to the sink to clean it so she didn't have to see her mother's hopeful expression.

"Anyone I know?" Her mother plunked her moped helmet down onto the kitchen counter that served as Mia's table and dropped onto a barstool beside it.

"Depends." Mia let the water run over the paintbrush and her fingers, remembering the way the ocean waves had rushed over her body that night on Seth's boat. "If I tell you, will you broadcast the news to Grammie and Grandpa in order to show them you know more about me than they do?"

When the expected spluttered gasps of indignation and teasing protest never came, Mia shut off the water and faced her mother.

Noelle frowned. "Is that what I do?"

"Don't you?"

"I don't know." She frowned harder.

Mia sighed. Her mother honestly never meant any harm. Noelle just wasn't a very introspective person and she didn't spend much time thinking about how her actions might hurt someone else.

"I'm meeting Seth," Mia admitted, figuring by confessing her secret she would atone for possibly hurting her mother's feelings.

"That's what I was afraid of," Noelle admitted, taking Mia by surprise. "You really like him, don't you?"

Mia wiped off her palette, not ready to quit work for the day, but wanting to organize and clean up just a little before Seth arrived.

"It's nothing serious. But I thought you'd be happy I was seeing someone."

"Oh, I am!" Noelle rose to walk around Mia's canvas, her frown downgrading into an all-out scowl. "More power to you, hon, if you like him. I just thought maybe if you *didn't* like him, he might hop back on his boat so he and his overbearing uncle would sail back into the sunset.''

''Seth's uncle?''

''Brock Chandler, the longshoreman with an ego to match his shoulders.''

''We have longshoremen in Florida?'' Mia mixed a new shade of red for Little Red Riding Hood, suddenly too distracted to finish cleaning up. Painting would occupy her, keep her from getting too nervous. ''Don't tell me you're having man trouble with a guy you've known for all of one day again.''

Her mother had been on a good streak over the past year, sticking around to help out the family, not being romanced by every stray sailboarder to stroll up out of the surf.

''Is that what you think of me, Mia? Honestly?'' An uncharacteristic strain of hurt threaded through the words. Noelle swiped her helmet back off the counter and dropped it on her head. ''I can count on one hand the guys who have given me trouble in this lifetime—Brock is one, and your father was the other. Trust me, every other man has been ruthlessly controlled and shoved aside so as not to piss off your grandfather or give Grandma any more reasons not to let me see you.'' Her voice thrummed with strong emotions her mother rarely—make that *never* until right now—vented.

''Um.'' Mia searched for the appropriate response before her mother tore out the front door and out of Twin Palms for another five years. ''Sorry?''

Noelle rolled her eyes, the melodramatic touch a

sure signal she was cooling down already. "Don't pretend an apology you don't feel, Mia. I'd ten times rather you say what you think than be forced to play happy shop girl for me all day."

Mia felt her eyebrows raise. In unison. Dark sarcasm was another tool Noelle Quentin hadn't often employed before. Obviously, Mia should have given more credence to Noelle's claim of man trouble.

"This uncle—he's the guy Seth showed up with at the store with this morning?"

"He kissed me!" Noelle punched one hand into the cushions of Mia's orange Art Deco sofa to accentuate the statement.

"And you're mad because you let him or mad because you aren't kissing him anymore?" Mia was totally out of her element. Although she'd heard stories of Noelle's adventures in dating from Grammie—no doubt a bit inflated, she now realized—Noelle had never actually shared that sort of thing with Mia before.

"I'm mad he made me kiss him in the first place and even more mad—"

"You liked it." Funny, in the space of two seconds, Mia now knew exactly what her mother was talking about. "I hear you. I'm rather furious with myself for enjoying Seth's kiss, too, but my newest strategy is to go with the flow and see what happens."

Noelle's jaw dropped. "Meaning?"

The doorbell rang again before Mia could come up with a response. She settled for a meaningful waggling of her eyebrows as she opened the door.

The worried frown on Noelle's face rated highly satisfying. After all, it was usually Mia who went around worrying and frowning and fretting about everyone in the family. Tonight, just once, she would be the one taking chances and living on the edge.

"COME ON IN." Mia's gaze met his, steady and sure, as she opened the oversize door to her converted boathouse.

Seth scarcely resisted the urge to punch one fist in the air with that small victory. He'd been convinced she'd change her mind before tonight, even going so far as to avoid his cell phone all day just in case she'd left him a message.

Before he had a chance to cross the threshold, however, Mia's mother charged past him down the front steps. She cast him a smile only slightly less frosty than those Mia's grandmother had given him this morning once she realized he was the pirate from Mia's wild weekend.

"Your grandpa told me to tell you that inventory starts at 5:00 a.m. sharp," Noelle shouted over one shoulder, the chin strap of her helmet swinging in time with her step. "Don't be late!"

There were obviously more family dynamics at work here than Seth could understand.

"Don't mind her," Mia offered, still holding the front door open. "She's always cranky when she hangs out at the store too long."

Seth gladly traded his focus from mother to daughter. Noelle might be annoyed that Seth showed up tonight, but Mia obviously wasn't.

So far so good. "You look great."

She wore a black men's dress shirt spotted with paint and short denim skirt with hearts sewn all along the hem. Her dark hair swung loose about her shoulders and she carried a much-splattered palette in one hand. A tiny smudge of red paint stained her cheek.

Unable to resist an opportunity to touch her, Seth wiped the splotch with his thumb.

Her cheeks flushed another shade of red in the wake of that light contact. Her fingers smoothed over her own skin, imitating his action.

"I sort of forget myself when I'm working." She backed up a step, allowing him room to enter her house.

"Can I see what you're doing?" Seth noted the high ceilings, the loft built into one end of the structure that was once clearly meant to house a couple of boats. This narrow old boathouse had probably been replaced by the marina's new sprawling building out front—a virtual boat condominium that could accommodate at least twenty-five watercraft.

"Only if you promise to keep any negative opinions to yourself." She smiled while she said it, but Seth caught the seriousness in her green cat eyes. "I don't mind thoughtful criticism once I'm done, but when I'm in the middle of creating something, it sort of upsets the process to get outside points of view."

"I'm definitely not an art critic. The only paintings I've spent much time perusing are the ones they use in the Sunday comics. Me and *Andy Capp* go way back." He followed her through the open living area and around a bizarre orange sofa with a diagonal backrest and no arms. His limited artistic knowledge pegged the sparse furnishings as Art Deco pieces, and he only knew that because he'd seen rooms like this on his occasional business treks to Miami Beach.

"Andy Capp?" She skirted an easel positioned in front of a window to sit on a tarp spread on the floor. "Don't get me wrong, I like *Andy Capp* as much as the next girl, but you look like a guy with more highbrow tastes."

"Trust me, after reading the *Wall Street Journal* from front to back every day, it's pretty refreshing to pick up the local paper and see where *Beetle Bailey* left off." He waited on the opposite side of the easel from her, not wanting to spoil the surprise of seeing her work for the first time.

Mia's gaze narrowed. "I can see the pirate liking the funnies. It's the corporate shark I can't picture engrossed in the *Family Circus.*"

"Well I *do* spend more time looking at Miss Buxley than Ditto, Dot and Chip," he admitted. "But right now I'd like to see what you've got going on over there on the easel." He pointed to the canvas still facing away from him. "May I?"

She dropped her palette onto a low worktable beside her and nodded.

Seth didn't know what sort of artwork he'd expected from this wild woman turned responsible family member and aspiring artist. But it definitely wasn't the fairy-tale extravaganza he discovered on her canvas.

Hansel and Gretel romped with Jack and the Beanstalk. Little Red Riding Hood picked apples in the forest with Snow White while the witches, giants and other assorted villains sat around a chess table in the background.

"Wow." He stepped closer, drawn by the vivid colors, the ornate details on everything from the woodsman's axe to the candy corns decorating a witch's candy house. "It's beautiful, Mia. What does it mean?"

"Mean?" She laughed, studying the canvas as if hoping to figure it out for herself. "I have no idea. Maybe we can wait until the critics look at it and read the reviews afterward."

"You must have had certain artistic intentions as you started it," Seth pressed, intrigued.

"I just wanted to make something pretty, something visually interesting." She shrugged, the careless gesture disrupting the length of hair that had been resting there. The silky brown locks slithered behind her. "I don't know where I got the idea for a fairy-tale compilation, but I started with that little pig in the left-hand corner and then just went crazy."

"I can't imagine wading into such a big project without a plan." He searched the canvas from one side to the other, continually finding something new.

She poked him in the ribs. "No negative commentary, remember?"

"I'm not suggesting that's a bad thing. It's a bold move and you made it pay off." He studied the face of a villainess—a figure bearing a striking resemblance to Mia's mother. "Isn't that your mom?"

"She's cast as a token wicked stepmother." Mia

flashed him an unrepentant grin. "She'll appreciate the imagery, I think."

"And what's Gretel up to over here?" Seth had thought she was climbing the Beanstalk with Jack and Hansel, but on second glance, she seemed to be straddling a small sapling bent at an awkward angle toward the ground.

"She's creating a catapult." Mia twisted a lock of brown hair with one finger, gazing at the painting beside him. "I sort of envisioned her sailing through the forest in search of her own adventures."

No sooner had the words slipped from her mouth than she ceased the hair twisting. Her finger lingered in midair while the silky brown strands slid back into place with the rest of her hair.

Her mouth curled into a silent, surprised *O,* the perfect position to receive his kiss, but Seth was determined to hear what she had to say about this intriguing development with Gretel.

"I mean, lots of people go out seeking adventures." She tugged at the collar of her oversize shirt, giving Seth a glimpse of a little more golden skin. "It's a common enough fairy-tale image to undertake a quest."

Seth wanted to see more of that creamy flesh, uncover more layers of the complicated woman in front of him.

He stepped closer, purposely crowding her. "Meaning Gretel's determination to be a wild child isn't in any way reflective of your own adventurous nature, right?"

"Right," she agreed entirely too quickly, her

breathing quick and light and very apparent from the rapid rise and fall of her blouse. "I'm much more grounded than she is," Mia continued, backing into the worktable full of paint behind her. "She's practically ready to fly away for the sake of adventure, but not me."

"No?" Seth laid one finger in the open vee of her shirt, stroked the smooth, heated skin of her throat down to her collarbone. He leaned closer, whispered words into the sweet luxury of her sable hair. "You may not be ready to fly away, but maybe if I'm very good to you, you'll fly apart for me tonight."

She shivered—shuddered, really—her whole body trembling with the force of that thought. Hell, his whole body strained toward her like an engine at full throttle and he hadn't even kissed her yet.

"Will you do that for me, Mia?" The heat between them swelled, surged. It didn't matter that there were windows open the whole height of the house. The mild ocean breeze didn't begin to cool the fire. "Will you let me help you find the best kind of adventure?"

DAMN THE MAN.

Mia struggled for a breath, fighting the wave of wanting Seth Chandler could inspire with nothing more than a fingertip.

And a few volcanic words.

Ever since he'd walked through her front door she'd been dreaming of wrapping herself around that tanned, muscular body. Sure his polo shirt and pleated shorts weren't any different from the trappings worn by most successful Florida businessmen on the weekends, but in her mind's eye, she still saw him with an eye patch.

She was plagued by memories of how good he looked without his shirt. Harassed by the knowledge that he called to her senses in the most primitive way, leaving her more hot and bothered than she'd ever been in her life.

By now she was set to go off like a rocket—coiled and ready to come undone for him just like he'd asked. She didn't stand a chance of turning him away tonight.

Despite her grandfather's ulcer, her mother's obvious displeasure and Mia's own logical arguments against having a torrid affair with Seth, she found herself caving to temptation. Fast.

But that didn't mean Mia had to let him call the shots.

If she was going to spend the night with Seth against her better judgment, she was at least going to stay in charge of the situation. And for starters, Mia couldn't let her senses get the best of her again, not after her surprising reaction to him that night on the boat. She was determined to remain in control for as long as she possibly could and see just how far her she could stretch her erotic endurance.

Seth wasn't the only one capable of plotting sensual adventures.

"I don't think we want me to lose control any time soon." Slowly, she walked her fingers onto the worktable behind her, trying not to notice the light brush of Seth's hand as he deftly unfastened the first button on her blouse. "You know the old adage about good things coming to those who wait?"

"Wait?" His fingers paused over the next button. Intense brown eyes watched her, confused. "It may kill me to walk away tonight, Mia, but if you really want me to wait, I will."

"No. I definitely don't want you to walk away." At least not until they were both feeling a lot more satisfied. "I want you to help me keep my senses at bay tonight until the last possible second. And while I'm delaying my natural inclinations to indulge *my* senses, I want to enflame *yours* to the limit."

Her voice wavered just a little as she confided her secret hope. But as she gripped the hidden item in one hand behind her back, her anticipation grew, heated, practically exploded inside her.

Seth's finger dipped farther into the open neck of her blouse, disappearing into the hollow between her breasts to tug at the lace of her bra. The slight invasion drew her nipples to hard, pointed peaks. An answering sensation tripped through her veins to that most sensitive spot between her thighs.

"A bold plan," he admitted, skimming a kiss across her cheek, fanning minty breath over her cheek. "But I wonder how you're going to manage that when you're so hot right now you could go into meltdown with a single, well-placed touch?"

As if to illustrate his point, Seth traced his finger in a circular motion on the soft underside of her breast. Her nipples ached with the wanting of that touch.

Her panties itched her thighs, chafed her hips and made her wriggle with the need to be naked.

Mia bit her lower lip, hard. "You don't know how committed I am to my course." With a great deal of effort, she dragged open eyes that had somehow closed without her permission. "And I have a secret weapon to help keep you in line." She gripped the weapon of choice until the smooth wood hurt her palm. "A tool guaranteed to wreak sensual pleasure and drive you as close to the edge as I am right now."

Seth lifted one lazy eyebrow, a smile playing about his full lips. "What are you hiding back there?"

He reached for the hand she'd kept tucked behind her back. His chest connected with her breasts as he leaned over her, sending a tide of sharp longing through every nerve. The nubby waffle-weave of his polo shirt seemed like provocative torture against the thin cotton of her blouse. The hard length of an obvious erection pressed against her thigh and nearly sent her straight out of her skin.

Desperate for distance before she forgot her good intentions, Mia willingly produced her seductive aid.

"A paintbrush?" Seth's voice failed to hide his skepticism.

Mia trailed the silky bristles over the strong column of his throat. "I've decided I'm going to paint you."

His dark brow furrowed. Clearly, the poor guy thought she'd lost her marbles.

"I don't know, Mia—"

"Nude."

The formerly furrowed brows shot up into his forehead. Of course, his mild shock didn't seem to diminish the impressive new dimensions of his body outlined by his shorts.

A new kind of pleasure pulsed through Mia. A playful pleasure that seemed to revel in tormenting Seth. She never knew passion could be this much fun.

"Why don't we wait until after—"

"No arguments, sailor." She leaned close to him, having gained enough cool that she now braved a provocative brush of her breasts up against his chest. The feeling was immediately divine, but Mia maintained control by thinking of all the ways she could drive Seth to the brink tonight.

"If we're going to have any fun," she whispered, her voice low and breathy. "I need you to get naked for me. Now."

9

CARMEN HAD RETURNED.

With a vengeance.

Seth gauged Mia's expression, more than a little surprised that aloof and elusive Mia Quentin had propositioned to paint him naked. But it sounded just like the sort of sexy stunt Carmen, Seducer of Unsuspecting Pirates, would pull.

"I don't know what kind of subject I'll make." He unfastened two more of her shirt buttons before she realized what he was doing and slapped his hands away.

The hell of it was, while he'd been slyly unbuttoning her blouse, she'd been twice as sly unfastening his belt.

He had to have been temporarily insane to have resisted this woman that night on his boat.

"You won't be the subject," she whispered, tugging his shirt up his chest until he gave in and pulled it over his head. "You're going to be the canvas."

His passion-fogged brain struggled to figure out what exactly that meant until she swiped her paintbrush in one broad stroke across his bare chest.

Bright blue paint remained as evidence of its passing.

"You're painting *me*." Understanding kicked in about the same moment as an all-new wave of lust.

Carmen's green eyes roved his body with obvious satisfaction. In one hand, she held her paintbrush, still slowly dripping onto the heavy tarp below them. In the other hand, she held a small can of blue paint.

"Are you taking off those shorts, sailor, or are you thinking about going noble on me again tonight?"

Seth replayed that question once in his mind, but even after double-checking, he still came up with the same interpretation. In the male playbook, that was called permission to tackle.

Mia's squeal of surprise didn't deter him in the least. Nor did the blue paint that went flying all over both of them as he lowered one shoulder into her belly and snowplowed her—relatively gently—onto the tarp.

The only thing he cared about at the moment was taking this conversation horizontal.

"I don't want to be in the painting," she protested, laughing and wriggling underneath him.

"Too bad." He wrestled the paintbrush out of her hand, then stroked the blue-coated bristles down her neck and into the hollow between her breasts. "You're not the only one who can play tormentor here."

Her eyes fluttered for a moment, her smile slipped as her jaw dropped and her back arched.

Fascinated, Seth swept aside her blouse and continued to brush downward over her golden skin until her abdomen was completely blue.

An ocean breeze blew through the high windows,

tickling their damp skin with salty air. Night sounds of the small town beach community drifted in along with it. Shouts and laughter from far away beach-goers as they walked their dogs or lit the bonfires they weren't supposed to have but always managed to ignite anyway.

An awareness of their surroundings—including every little nuance of Mia's warm skin next to his—seeped into his consciousness.

Including the very hot center of her straddling one of his thighs.

He understood she wanted to draw things out, slow things down tonight. But there was only so much a man could bear when such strong…enticement rested this close to him.

"You're wicked," she half moaned, half sighed.

"I was just thinking the same thing." He met no resistance as he reached behind her to unclasp her bra, then pushed the straps down each of her shoulders. A fierce shudder made her whole body shimmy against his.

"No. Mild-mannered artists are no match for wild-eyed pirates in the wicked department." She smoothed her fingers over his cheek, combed her nails through his hair and down the back of his neck.

"Don't underestimate your Carmen alter ego." He cupped her breast in his hand, teased the nipple with his thumb. "But I promise not to be wicked anymore."

Her green eyes opened, heavy-lidded with sultry heat, but curious. "No?"

"I plan to be very, very nice." He lowered his

mouth to her breast for a taste. "And I promise to draw things out for just as long as you like. All night, if that's what you want."

Mia heard Seth's words, but they failed to make sense in a brain that had gone on autopilot ever since he'd wrestled her to the floor.

She wanted him. Right here, right now, and damn the consequences. And as for drawing things out? She couldn't stand to wait three more seconds let alone all night.

The bravado she'd experienced earlier with her paintbrush in hand had vanished once they'd stretched out on the tarp. Now, with her blood slamming through her veins with each pound of her heart and her nerve endings taut and tingling with want, the only thing she could think about was having his hands all over her, his body deep inside hers.

"I don't want to wait."

His mouth licked a slow path down her belly to what would no doubt be an erotic experience she'd never forget. But she couldn't wait. "Please."

He paused, glancing up at her from a position above her thighs guaranteed to make any woman's temperature spike a few degrees. In fact, Mia hovered near the boiling point and she didn't want to hit that peak without him there to share it with her.

"I thought I could wait, but you make me so—" She leaned forward to kiss him so she wouldn't have to finish the sentence. He had to know what he did to her anyway. She probably scratched him in her haste to help him out of his shorts.

Her nipples burned, her breasts ached. She wriggled out of her skirt, flung her panties to the far corner of the room and pulled him closer.

The hot tip of him touched her in the most intimate spot possible. She reached for him, wanting to stroke him with her hand, but he seized her wrist before she had the chance.

"You're not the only one wound too tight." His words grazed her ear as he nuzzled her neck, kissed her throat, licked a path toward her shoulder.

She didn't need to ask if he had protection. The kiss they'd shared this afternoon had been like a flashing neon warning of things to come—they'd both known if they got close again they wouldn't be able to stop themselves from taking their relationship to the next level.

And Seth Chandler wasn't the kind of man to walk in the door without a plan.

She waited for the joining her body wanted so badly. She was surprised to hear Seth's voice above her instead.

"I want more than tonight, Mia." He held himself over her by all of an inch. His arms bracketed her shoulders, leveraging his body off hers with a low push-up.

She'd never seen such perfect biceps.

"Do you know what I'm saying?" he asked, his voice serious, intent.

She had no clue. Was she supposed to be responsible for thinking right now?

"I'm not going anywhere tomorrow," he explained, his pecs flexed and delicious and a hair's breadth from her breasts. "Or the next day."

He lowered himself a fraction of an inch closer, making argument impossible. Mia would think of a way to deal with the fallout later.

Right now, she needed this. Him.

His mouth landed on hers the same moment he edged himself inside her. His body should have pressed hers into the stiff canvas tarp beneath them, but she felt so warm and liquid under him, around him, she seemed to accommodate him in every way. The delicious sensation of being taken over, of utterly losing control, was sweeter than she could have ever imagined.

Never had she given herself to a man like this. Never had she experienced such a fierce sense of possessing and being possessed.

They rolled across the tarp, exchanging positions of dominance, gaining and relinquishing sensual power. The spilled contents of the blue paint can coated their limbs, their backs, their bellies. Mia slid, slipped and sighed her way to one tense sexual peak after another only to return to a higher, more urgent place the next time.

Not until she pleaded with Seth for release, threatening vengeance with her paintbrush, did he push her over that final ledge. She catapulted her way into a spiral of sweet satisfaction, wringing his surrender from him at the same time.

When she regained enough energy to lift her head, she stared down at the war-painted pirate beneath her, only to discover a wicked grin on his face.

"You have a way with adventure, woman."

She wouldn't have thought it possible for that sexy

smile to turn her on all over again. At least not yet. But already, she wanted to taste him, tease him, tempt him all over again.

As another sultry gust of ocean air drifted in through the windows to fan their bodies, Mia let her inner Carmen do the talking for her.

"And to think, that was only just the beginning."

SETH WOKE just before five. No matter that he'd hardly slept all night in his headlong rush to provide Mia with every conceivable sexual escapade she could ever envision. His head was instantly clear, ready to take on the day.

The curse of being raised a fisherman, maybe. Even before his father walked out for good, Seth had grown accustomed to going out before dawn to fish. If nothing else, he could at least provide dinner, but on a good day he could make a few bucks by selling whatever he caught to a dockside market.

He'd never waken his brother, Jesse, or his sister, Christine, to go out with him. They had always volunteered to help, but somehow it seemed cruel to roll his siblings out of bed at 4:00 a.m. on a school day.

And he wouldn't wake Mia now, either. He walked silently around the loft that served as her bedroom, and downstairs to retrieve his paint-spattered clothes. They'd taken a shower together at one point last night, so at least the rest of him was clean.

He let himself out of the boathouse and jogged down the pier toward the slip where Brock's boat was docked. He would go back to Mia's as soon as he retrieved some clean clothes. No doubt she'd appreciate it if he didn't walk out of her house at 9:00 a.m. wearing rumpled, splotched clothes from the day before.

Besides, he needed to talk to her about where things stood with them. Their night together had solidified something between them and he wanted to make sure she understood that. He'd never been the kind of man to indulge in a one-night relationship and he sure as hell wouldn't walk away from a woman.

That meant they had some serious talking to do.

Seth found his clothes, but no trace of Brock. He brushed his teeth and changed in the dark, not wanting to attract the attention of anyone who might be up and about this early in Twin Palms.

He was halfway back to the boathouse when he heard the sounds of Big Band Tunes emanating from Mia's place. He smelled coffee as he opened the door. Smiling to himself that he'd found a woman who was an early riser too, Seth headed for the kitchen—the only room with lights on—to see if he could entice her into sharing the best early morning delight of all.

Their night together had been so good it was almost scary. A fact which Seth refused to think about in light of the fact that he wasn't the kind of man to ever walk away from a woman. Even if she did rock his whole damn universe.

He found her at the sink, tossing paintbrushes and palettes and old paint cans into a tub full of steaming water. Her hair coated her shoulders and her back in shiny brown silk. Here and there, a few strands full of static electricity danced of their own accord behind her.

She wore a purple T-shirt covered with blue butterflies that clung to her curves and barely met the waistband of her low-slung jean shorts.

He couldn't wait to get his hands on that smooth expanse of exposed skin.

With any luck, they could resolve things between them, agree on a few parameters for their relationship, and they'd be back in her bed in no time. For that matter, maybe they could discuss matters while they were *in* bed. *After* he'd touched that enticing slash of bare midriff....

Her voice iced that thought before he had a chance to act on it.

"If you think you can waltz in and out of my house, Seth Chandler, you've got another thing coming."

MIA WATCHED Seth's reaction, pleased she had at least taken him a little off guard. Served him right.

He'd caught her plenty off guard this morning when he had snuck right out of her bed and out the front door without so much as a "thanks, it's been nice."

No wonder she'd gotten along this far in life just fine without a man.

"I just wanted to grab some clean clothes." He stabbed a thumb in the air toward the water. Obviously he'd gone back to the boat.

Sure, it sounded reasonable enough, but how would he have liked to wake up alone?

"You might have told me." She wasn't about to forget her anger that easily. Especially not when she was so confused about what to do next. "Now half of Twin Palms probably knows we spent the night together. You can't just sneak around at 5:00 a.m. in a small town and not expect someone to see you, Seth. At this rate, my grandfather will be calling me any minute."

She turned back to the sink full of paintbrushes, wishing Seth hadn't made her feel so many things last night. All she wanted was to crawl back under the covers with him and not come out, but that wouldn't salvage her grandparents' business and it wouldn't do anything to further the art she loved.

Before she could think what to say next, Seth's hands settled around the bare skin at her waist, reminding her exactly how much she'd missed his touch in the half an hour they'd been apart.

"I'm sorry."

She could feel the heat from his chest, his arms, even though he still stood a few inches behind her. It would be so easy to lean back into his warmth, his strength. But then, would she be any different from her mother who had always relied on someone else to take care of her? Even relying on someone else to take care of her own daughter?

"But if the town knows about us," Seth continued, passing her a dishtowel to dry her hands, "it only saves us having to tell them. They were going to find out anyway."

Had she missed something here? "How would they have found out anyway?"

He crossed his arms over his chest and frowned. "If we're hanging out together and my car is parked in the driveway all the time, they're going to get the picture pretty fast, Mia."

"That's not going to happen, Seth." She folded her arms in perfect imitation of him, ready to take him on. "I don't know how we jumped from spending the night together to becoming something of an item, but I'm not ready to take that step."

She hadn't even managed to fully break free from her grandparents' dependence on her yet. There was so much she wanted to achieve on her own before she got involved with someone. A man like Seth would distract her. He'd already distracted her! She had a gallery showing next week and instead of spending last night working on her paintings she'd been rolling around in the watercolors with a sexy pirate who could turn her inside out with a few kisses.

"I told you last night this couldn't be a one-time thing." His intense brown eyes studied her, his jaw clenched between words. "That's why nothing happened between us on the boat. I thought you understood that."

She should have. She remembered Seth's words to her last night—*I'm not going anywhere tomorrow.* But didn't all men spout phrases like that in the heat of the moment?

"Do you mean to tell me you've *never* had a one-night stand?"

"The only women I've been with were serious relationships for me." His jaw quit clenching, his gaze broke away from hers to flit around the compact kitchen.

Something struck her as odd in his statement. Something she couldn't quite put her finger on yet.

"Define serious."

"Women I've lived with."

She didn't know what she'd expected him to say, but it hadn't been that. He'd only slept with women who had lived with him? She had to admit, that sounded pretty serious. And very honorable on his part.

But as long as they were getting down to brass tacks, she wanted to put the finest point possible on the situation.

"Not that it matters one way or another, but were these women you lived with but weren't engaged to?" Call her nosy. But damn it, was he honestly expecting her to conform to his ideal dating pattern here?

"I never got to that stage, no."

Interesting that cohabitation came before engagements these days. Not just once, either. "How many women are we talking exactly?"

He cursed. "I would never ask you how many guys you've been with, Mia."

She shrugged, unintimidated. He was the one who started this. "But I would fully expect to disclose how many guys I'd *lived* with. Now fess up. How many women have you pulled into the cohabitation scheme?"

"Five."

She felt her eyebrows shoot up into the nether

reaches of her forehead, but she couldn't seem to tug them back down. "Five?"

"Okay, so I'm not a monk. But five's not that many."

Not many for a thirty-something-year-old guy to have slept with, maybe. But for him to have *lived* with?

She pulled her brushes out of the water and dried them with the towel. Slowly. Buying herself thinking time.

She couldn't stand next to Seth for ten seconds without wanting him, but she wasn't ready for the kind of relationship he seemed to expect. Shoot, she couldn't see herself dating someone on a regular basis given the permanent crisis condition of her life. She sure as hell wasn't about to pack her easels to go live with a sexy corporate tycoon.

"I've got a lot going on in my life right now—"

"So let me help."

"Are you good with watercolors?" She offered him a paintbrush.

"What about the situation at the Beachcomber? Maybe I could—"

She jammed the handful of paintbrushes into a bucket on her worktable. "I don't want help, Seth. I want to figure out things for myself. But I liked being with you last night because I didn't have to worry or be stressed or think too hard. If you want to be with me for *me*—not because you want to fix things for me and not because you think I need a live-in protector—then come back and see me sometime."

It was the best she could offer, damn it. And it

was a far cry from booting him out of the boathouse, an option that had been her first, automatic inclination this morning when she was still scared to face the consequences of her night with him.

Seth juggled a clean paint can from hand to hand, contemplating her with those sexy brown eyes. Slowly he nodded. He backed toward the front door, keeping his eye on her the whole time.

"Okay." He quit juggling and gripped the can in one hand. "But I'm not going anywhere. Not tomorrow. And not the day after that."

His gaze flickered to the bucket of empty paint cans across the room by her feet, then he lined up his shot and sent his can sailing through the air to land with a clank in the center of the pail.

He winked at her as he let himself out. "You can count on it."

10

NOELLE COUNTED boxes of inflatable starfish pool toys in the Beachcomber's stockroom and marked the final tally on an inventory sheet Mia had given her the night before. Four days had passed since Brock Chandler stomped into her life with his fishing boots and the only way Noelle had survived his arrival had been to shoulder ever-increasing amounts of work at the Beachcomber.

The community college where she taught had been out on winter break all week, so she seemed to have no escape from the biggest temptation of her life. Not that a surly fisherman with big hands and a smile he seemed to reserve only for her should have been all that tempting. But something about Brock called to her on a primitive level that had nothing to do with logic or reason.

She moved on to counting inflatable ride-on alligators, wondering how much of this stuff Mia would keep when she restocked the store full of the new, more upscale inventory to complement the Beachcomber's updated look. Noelle's parents would probably have a conniption when they discovered Mia wanted to highlight products like natural sponges and high-end exfoliating sea salts in gift baskets rather than blow-up Shamus.

But then again, Betty and Norman had been a bit less feisty this week, a bit more resigned to the changes Mia wanted in the store. Their uncharacteristic relenting made Noelle realize how much she had always admired their fierce determination even though they could be the world's most stubborn pair.

If her parents hadn't been so determined, they might not have done such a good job raising Mia. And for all the grief Noelle gave them about their overprotectiveness and their rigid house rules, she had to admit, they'd done a great job.

Of course, she'd produced a great kid, damn it, and she wished her parents would admit that just once.

Climbing up on a wooden step stool to get a better view of the orange foam life preservers hanging from the rafters, Noelle heard the door behind her creak. Because her parents had driven to a hardware store in Tampa to pick up the new paint and flooring for the store, Noelle knew her guest could only be Mia.

But her daughter didn't fill out a doorframe half as impressively as her uninvited guest.

Brock stood in the harsh glare of the room's lone, undiluted lightbulb. His closely cropped dark brown hair was still damp from a shower. Curse his hide, he looked incredible.

"Thought you could use a cup of coffee." He held out a double-size paper cup from a doughnut shop up the street while she hopped off the step stool. "Actually it's that tutti-frutti stuff you like."

She knew exactly what it was by the fabulous smell already drifting through the stockroom. Her feet carried her toward Brock—not because of the allure of the man, she assured herself, but only because he came bearing just the right gift at 7:00 a.m. on a Saturday.

"How did you know I like chocolate hazelnut?" She took the cup gratefully, vaguely wishing she could grab Brock and drink him up, too.

Brock set his own steaming cup on an old butcher's table half-buried in boxes. "That's life in a small town for you. If you ask the doughnut shop girl for Noelle Quentin's regular order, she doesn't even blink."

Great. Sold out by her own neighbors. Noelle sipped the gourmet coffee and lied to herself that she owed the warmth churning through her veins to the beverage. "How did you know I was in here this morning?"

"So you admit you've been hiding from me?"

"I'm admitting nothing of the sort." Even though she'd absolutely been running from him like a cat at bath time. She had the sneaking suspicion—and downright fear—that if she let herself spend time with this magnetic man she'd lose the upper hand she needed to have in her relationships.

"I just can't imagine how you would have known I'd be in the stockroom on a Saturday at the crack of dawn when I normally keep as much distance between me and this place as possible."

Brock walked around the table to join her, making her heart speed up just a little with every step he took. Why hadn't she worn something besides this way-too-insubstantial tank top? She refused to cross her arms over her chest and hide, but the urge definitely niggled.

He peered over her shoulder at the inventory sheet and then frowned around at the boxes behind them.

"Seems to me you're here all the time." His eyes roamed up and down the stacks of boxes. "But this morning was a no-brainer because I was out fishing when the moped pulled up to the store."

Foiled again. "Don't you ever sleep?"

He ceased his careful perusal of the Beachcomber inventory to stare back at her. "That's one of the benefits of an older man, Noelle. We don't need much rest."

Noelle would have choked on her coffee had she been drinking any at that moment. She hastened to redirect the conversation as she warded off the temptation to fan herself. "Older? You can't be any older than me, buster, so watch who you're calling older."

"I'm forty-two and getting better with age." He plucked the inventory sheet and clipboard out of her hands and started jotting down numbers.

Heaven help her if he got any better than he was right now. The proximity of his body put her every nerve ending on intense alert.

She attempted to distract herself by peering over his shoulder to see what he scribbled on her paper.

His husky Bruce Springsteen voice seemed much too close. "You know, some of us figure out what we want as we get older and aren't afraid to go after it."

Noelle was so busy frowning at the numbers he'd filled in that she almost let that one slide by her. "Excuse me?" Was he intimating that she was afraid to go after *him?*

Brock totaled the columns for stuffed porpoises and pink plastic sand buckets. He paused to shoot her a meaningful look.

"I said, another nice thing about getting older is that *some of us* figure out what we want as we get older and aren't afraid to go after it." He leaned fractionally closer, as if illustrating exactly what he meant by that remark.

Of all the pompous, full-of-himself comments. Noelle fumed at his arrogance.

"Who said anything about wanting you, Brock Chandler? If I did, you can bet I wouldn't be the least bit afraid to jump your bones and make you forget your own damn name right here and now."

The twenty-year-old institutional clock on the wall ticked off three painstaking seconds in the silence that followed. Brock's patient gaze seemed to be envisioning that flagrant scenario in vivid detail.

Noelle barely resisted the urge to lick lips gone dry as the Beachcomber's cash flow.

"As enticing as that sounds, Noelle, I was actually referring to your hesitance to purchase that prime piece of beachfront real estate on the other side of the marina. *That's* what I was suggesting you should go after." He stroked his unshaven jaw with one big hand, as if still contemplating the jumping bones notion. "Although your idea has a certain merit, too."

How perfectly mortifying.

HOW KICK-ASS PERFECT.

Brock refused to allow himself the smile that itched the corners of his mouth. Thank God for the inventory sheet in front of him and the convenient excuse to look at rows of snooze-worthy numbers or he might have accidentally pumped a victorious fist and celebrated Noelle's slipup a bit too heartily.

She looked as gorgeous at 7:00 a.m. as she did any other time of day. Her loose ponytail and scrubbed cheeks weren't exactly the trademarks of a beauty queen, but Noelle had the most sexy, knowing green eyes he'd ever seen. When paired with the curvy enticement of her very hot body, Brock didn't stand a chance. Especially when said curves were covered with little more than a purple tank top and silky running shorts.

No way would he mess up his chance at a hot night with this sexy rebel and send her back underground again, not after how patient he'd been all week.

"Oh." Noelle sipped her coffee and pretended not to notice the electric sparks arcing between them. "Well I'm absolutely not going to tie up my savings right now, just in case Mia needs it for the mortgage on the Beachcomber. The business is really behind in its payments, a situation I would remedy if I could, but Mia refuses to let me help and continues to make me feel like an outsider in my own family."

Brock set his pen and the inventory sheet aside, intrigued by this new information. Noelle hadn't shared much of anything with him outside of a single, reluctant kiss that had turned into the hottest, fantasy-inducing mating of tongues he'd ever experienced.

And he'd only managed that much out of blackmail.

For her to share some part of herself with him now pleased him to no end, even if she imparted the news in an effort to lead him away from their former, enticing topic of conversation.

"She doesn't do it on purpose, of course," Noelle clarified, leaning one curvy hip against the butcherblock table as they talked. One of the straps on her tank top shifted down her shoulder just a little as she moved, begging Brock's hand to readjust it. Or slip it the rest of the way off....

Noelle's voice dragged him back to focus on her words. "Mia's just adamant that Beachcomber either fly or die on its own. But the thing that bugs me is that she gets to pour her own funds into the confounded money pit of a store. Why can't I?"

"Maybe she wants to prove something to herself. Isn't that the guiding principle for each generation— to establish they don't need parental help, advice or opinions?"

"She can't be trying to prove that to me," Noelle huffed, idly tugging the shoulder strap back into place. "I'm still in the process of proving that to my own parents."

Brock wasn't going there. Noelle's relationship with the elder Quentins looked strained to the most casual observer, and she probably wouldn't thank him for sharing his own, admittedly uninformed, view of that particular standoff. "I only meant to suggest you ought to buy that property and follow your own dreams, Noelle. Space like that doesn't become available every year, and with that location, it's not going to stay on the market long.''

"But the Beachcomber might need the money." Noelle snatched up the inventory sheet and approached the boxes again, obviously attempting to close the discussion.

Brock, however, had never been one to take a hint.

"Mia isn't going to accept your money." He inserted himself between her and the damn boxes, determined to make her listen. "You might actually help her a lot more by opening another business down here and driving more traffic past her updated storefront. All of Twin Palms could benefit from the extra tourist draw of a place like the one you have in mind."

She stared down at her stupid inventory-in-triplicate forms, doing a damn good job of ignoring him. He might have backed away if not for the fast blink of her green eyes, the hot tension between them so thick he could almost reach out and touch it.

"I don't know who you think you are to barge in here and tell me how to run my life," she returned after an endless moment of electric silence. "But I don't like it one bit."

"No? Then how come I don't see you walking away, Noelle?" If ever there'd been a moment to press his suit, that moment was now. He'd been waiting for a way to bait her, a way to maneuver around her glaring, don't-you-dare defenses. "Is it because you're too busy envisioning ways to make me forget my own damn name this morning?''

The glare she shot him looked two steps away from murderous.

''You don't see me walking away because this is my life, my town, my business and my Saturday morning to take inventory.'' Her cheeks flushed, her eyes shone and she leaned a fraction closer to him as she got in his face to make the point.

Slowly, she rolled up her handful of papers and stabbed him in the chest with one end of the roll. ''You're the one who needs to walk away, and if you had any ideas about putting the moves on me today, you'd better take them with you when you go. I've seen every trick in the book, hotshot, and I'm not about to have my head turned at this point in my life.''

Brock curled one hand around the rolled up papers and slid them out of her grip to set them on the table behind her in the overcrowded stockroom. Deprived of her weapon, she didn't look quite so fierce.

She looked downright provocative, in fact, with that high color still staining her cheeks, her lips parted and her breath catching in erratic little huffs.

Instinct told him he could kiss her now and get away with it. Hell, he could probably kiss her until next week and get away with it. But he wanted more than a few mind-drugging nights from this woman, and if that meant waiting until she came to him on her own terms, he would damn well cool his heels. And his X-rated thoughts.

He hoped.

"I'm not going to put the moves on you today, Noelle," he confided, edging her backward until her hip bumped the big table in the middle of the crowded stockroom. "But I guarantee you, if I did, I would have a trick you haven't seen before."

Her green eyes narrowed. "You think so?"

He braced his palms on a tall box resting on the table behind her to bracket her body with his arms. The vague scents of soap and something citrusy teased his nose. He didn't dare touch her. Not unless he wanted to forget all of his noble intentions of all or nothing with her. If her soft skin so much as grazed him now he was toast.

"I know so, sweetheart. Because I'll bet my boat the only trick you haven't seen is no tricks at all. No trappings, no candlelight, no lingerie, no leather and no damned whipped cream. Just you and me and the sound of our breathing."

Her eyes widened, pupils dilated until he could hardly see the rim of green around the outside. Her soft gasp nearly undid him.

He clenched his teeth against the surge of lust, tightening his hands to fists on the cardboard box behind her.

"Just your bare legs wrapped around my waist, me pushing myself inside you and you crying out like the room is on fire." That last image was wrenched right out of the dream that had woken him this morning. His voice downgraded to barely a growl at the thought. "But then again, when you and I get together Noelle, the damn room probably will be."

His dumb-ass plan called for him to walk away right now to let her think about that particular little newsflash.

But Brock didn't have a chance in hell of moving so much as a millimeter away from her. Every nerve—and God knew, every blood vessel—strained toward her with an insistence he had no hope of denying.

He might have battled against his own urges for another minute—or at least ten seconds—but then Noelle flung herself at him with a strength he hadn't come close to suspecting. Her arms wound around his neck, her tall, curvy body glued itself to his with fierce determination, her fingers threaded through his hair and pulled his lips right down to hers with far more hunger than finesse.

And it was ten times more perfect than any lame dream he could have concocted.

Everything about her was smooth and fluid, warm and welcoming. Her breasts molded to his chest, scorched his T-shirt with their gently rounded shape, barely disguised by the thin material of her tiny purple tank top. Her lips parted for him instantly.

She tasted like chocolate hazelnut but hotter—slippery and sweet and so good he couldn't begin to get enough. His hands roamed her satiny skin, smoothed over her shoulders and down her arms to the indentation of her waist.

He squeezed her hips, pulled her closer, drove himself insane. He needed her now, wanted to take her right here in the cramped confines of the tiny storage room, but somehow that didn't sound like the scenario he'd promised her.

"Come to the boat," he whispered the words, hoarse and rough, into her ear.

"Here," she whispered back, mouthing the words onto his neck as she licked her way to his shoulder for a soft bite. "Now."

Five more seconds and he would have caved. He'd wanted her since the first second he'd seen her, knew he wanted her forever since she'd tried to run away from him on a moped, of all things.

But before he could clear the table for a thorough inventory of Noelle Quentin's gorgeous body, a bell rang from out in the front part of the store.

Noelle froze, her white teeth still bared and poised over his shoulder, her hands still stuffed inside his shirt. From inside the tourist shop, Seth's voice mingled with Mia's and floated toward the back room.

Noelle pulled away like she'd just been burned, her hands smoothing through her hair and tugging at the straps of her tank top.

"Come to the boat," Brock insisted, a sinking feeling in his gut telling him Noelle would use this opportunity to run.

She jumped around the tiny space, retrieving her papers, finding her coffee cup, fanning herself thoroughly. At least the last part was slightly encouraging.

"I can't," she told him, not even bothering to look in his direction. "Ill-conceived plan. Bad attack of hormones. Can't talk now."

Mia's voice grew louder as she obviously neared the back room.

"So talk to me at the boat. Or we can go to your place."

Noelle shook her head so fast her hair danced a crazy shimmy all over her shoulders. "No. I'm not the wild and willing chick of my youth anymore. I'm not jumping any bones, and I'm definitely not letting you try out the trick of no tricks." Her hands shook ever so slightly on the inventory paper, her voice scarcely more than a whisper. "I mean it, Brock. I can't do this."

Before he could argue the point, she plowed through the door to the store, greeting Seth and Mia by launching into a tale of her inventory woes as if she hadn't just been two seconds away from giving herself to him on a butcher-block table in the back room.

Brock scrubbed a hand across his face and wished he could scavenge up a scrap of the patience he'd sworn he had cultivated at some point in his life. But find it he would, because there wasn't a chance he was letting Noelle Quentin slip away from him now.

SETH STARED at Noelle's flushed cheeks and tousled hair and knew something was amiss. Something bigger than her struggle with the inventory sheets she waved around. Still, Mia's mother rattled on, oblivious to the tension in the room growing thicker by the minute between him and Mia.

He stole a glance at Mia across the store where she stood running one hand over the brackets for new shelving, looking sexy as hell in a pink T-shirt and matching running shorts. She'd ignored him ever since he descended on her outside the Beachcomber, angling to spend some time with her.

He'd sent her orchids this week. Right after he'd decorated her front door with a new jasmine vine growing in a pot shaped like a gingerbread house. He kept hoping a few extra gifts would entice her inner Gretel out for more adventures.

But so far, to no avail. She wanted no part of a relationship she perceived as too serious, and insisted she needed to pursue her own goals and dreams. Why couldn't she pursue her dreams with him by her side?

Luckily, he'd never backed down from a challenge.

"Are either of you listening to me at all?" Noelle's irritated voice sliced through his thoughts, calling him back from idle contemplation of Mia's mile-long legs in running shorts.

Mia moved away from the brackets to field the question. "Sorry, Mom. Seth and I were just having a bit of a disagreement so we're a little distracted."

Seth admired a woman who didn't hedge around the truth. But he couldn't let Mia put her spin on it without at least adding his two cents. "Disagreement? I thought we were compromising toward a solution."

Brock stepped from the back room before Mia could protest.

"Here, here," he called from the doorframe, lifting a cup of coffee in salute. "Compromise is key in a good relationship."

Seth nodded. Damn it, how come modern men understood this while the women hemmed and hawed and pointed to the lives they wanted to pursue?

Noelle unleashed a growl to halt all talk of compromise, however. "That does it." She slammed her paperwork on the Beachcomber's checkout counter and grabbed Mia by the elbow.

"You men can pound your chests and congratulate yourselves on the art of compromise all you want." She linked her arm through Mia's. "We're out of here for some major girl talk and there's not a damn thing you can do to stop us."

Seth watched in mild surprise as Mia and her mother seemed to agree on something for the first time all week. The Quentin women barreled out of the Beachcomber without so much as a glance behind them.

"What do you think they're doing?" Seth had to ask. His uncle didn't seem to have a clue when it came to women, but Brock *had* managed to woo the moped-riding rebel of Twin Palms, and that counted for something.

"They're trying to figure out how to get us the hell out of town." Brock joined him at the front door of the empty, gutted store to stare out at Mia and Noelle as they crossed the patch of sandy driveway toward Mia's converted boathouse.

Seth whistled under his breath. "I don't know about you, but I'm sleeping with one eye open until we're on firmer footing here."

Brock shook his head. "Those women will have you on the first boat back to Tampa, kid. Don't sleep."

11

HALF AN HOUR LATER, Mia began the comforting ritual of mixing paints inside her boathouse while Noelle still ranted and raved about Brock Chandler.

"You know what he does for a living?" Noelle asked from her perch on the floor where she brushed fresh wood stain onto an antique sideboard Mia had slated for the renovated Beachcomber.

Mia remained silent, struggling to center herself as she poured more blue into the lavender she was mixing. Noelle would provide the answer no matter what Mia might have to say, and Mia's mind remained too preoccupied with thoughts of Seth.

"He operates a charter boat when he's not fishing or taking people out for a tour of the Bay," Noelle supplied, her brush moving across the scarred wood with frightening speed. "Now what kind of career is that?"

"Sounds like the kind of career you would have loved," Mia answered honestly. She hadn't gotten to spend too much time with Seth's gruff uncle, but she liked what she'd seen of him. He wasn't much for idle conversation, but he'd won over Mia's grandfather from day one, and Mia had to appreciate that.

Grandpa never liked men around his daughter or

granddaughter. For that matter, Norman didn't usually like *anyone*. But one look at all Brock's cool fishing equipment, and he'd started liking Brock. So much so that when Brock came around for a game of chess or to share a fishing tale, Grandpa forgot all about his antacids.

Maybe the recent failure of the store was taking a bite out of his surliness.

"That's exactly the problem!" Noelle slapped her brush down onto the newspaper-covered floor. "I'm classically irresponsible. Why would I ever want a guy who fits my same profile? I like reserved, predictable guys."

"Oh please." Mia swirled her tiny paint stick around and around the paint can. "You like hellraisers, Mom. If anything, Brock is probably too boring for you, being a fisherman and all."

"Boring?" Noelle's jaw hung wide open. "Sweetheart, Brock Chandler is as far from boring as a man can get. I just don't think I should get caught up with a guy who doesn't have any more sense than me."

Brock seemed very possessed of good sense, but Mia kept her lips zipped. Noelle was obviously working through some issues here and Mia had no intention of getting involved in any minipsychology seminars.

"Let's face it," Noelle continued, plucking up her brush again. "This is when I ought to cut and run."

The words struck Mia oddly. The phrase about cutting and running echoed through her, replaying in her head.

"Cutting and running has never been a good approach, Mom," Mia found herself saying, her voice hoarse with emotions she hadn't been expecting, hadn't confronted in a long time.

Noelle's brush slowed, but did not stop. She stared hard at her project, as if the simple staining job was suddenly too difficult.

"I never wanted to cut and run without you, Mia," she said finally. "I let your grandparents convince me things would be better for you if I did, but I never *wanted* to do it."

"It doesn't matter." Those hurts were eons ago, and she'd found a comfortable friendship with her mother. Hadn't she?

"It does matter, damn it." Noelle tossed the brush back in the can of stain and crossed the floor to face Mia. "I'm sorry I wasn't strong enough to stand up to my parents then. I was good at rebelling—I wasn't so good at being reasonable." She reached to tuck a strand of Mia's hair behind one ear. "And they seemed to know what would be best for you so much better than I did."

"Grammie and Grandpa always seem to know best." Mia rolled her eyes, needing to take the conversation back to more familiar footing. "Still."

Noelle bit her lip, as if debating whether or not to say more, then turned on her heel and headed back to her refinishing project. "I don't know, Mia. Have you noticed they're getting frighteningly cooperative with the renovations lately? I almost fell over when they agreed to make the trek to the hardware store to pick up the paint and flooring today. I just hope they don't come back with flamingo wallpaper."

The same thought had occurred to Mia, but she'd been too distracted by a certain pirate-turned-financier to worry about it this morning.

Nope. She'd been too busy wondering how to hold fast and not give in to Seth's pursuit when he continued to cross her path everyday. It didn't help matters that half the time she saw him he wasn't wearing a shirt. The man went fishing without it, walked the boardwalk on the beach without it and rebuilt the Beachcomber's rickety front steps without it.

Did he live to torture her?

Next thing she knew she'd mixed way too much yellow into her orange and rendered a whole pot of paint useless. Frustrated with her inability to concentrate she turned on Noelle again.

"So what are you going to do about Brock?" Maybe her mother's struggle with a persistent, appealing man would give Mia some insights on what to do about Seth.

"I think I need to figure out my own life and my own problems before I try to figure out man trouble." Noelle's brush stopped, started, stopped again. "I know you don't think it's a good idea, but I'm going to walk away."

Was she blind? Brock obviously adored her. And he seemed to have ten times the substance of her usual men.

Maybe that's what scared Noelle.

"Well, shoot." Mia set aside the red and yellow paints and began working on her background instead. She'd mix the other colors later, when she wasn't so rattled.

"What?"

"You know I'm bound and determined not to follow in your footsteps." Mia slapped lavender paint on her canvas, glad to be working with the rich, true colors of oils again after the fairy-tale watercolors. "If you're not going to give Brock a chance, then I'm going to have to make an effort to work things out with Seth."

Noelle snorted. "Oh please. You've been pining for him for days. I'm just convenient permission to do what you wanted in the first place."

There might be a kernel of truth to that. Mia couldn't seem to stop remembering the night she and Seth had created the coolest painting of all—the blue imprints of their painted bodies forever stamped across her tarp on the floor. How could a woman focus on work with such a vivid reminder of stellar sex at her feet?

"Besides," Noelle continued, thankfully unaware of the turn Mia's thoughts had taken. "I think Brock has been singing Seth's praises to Grandpa on their fishing outings. I bet you're going to get the thumbs-up on your pirate after all."

Interesting. A man who wouldn't give Grandpa ulcers. A man who hadn't been afraid to stick around long enough to overcome her grandparents' gruff skepticism.

Seth was intriguing her more by the moment.

Her mind made up to see what happened with Seth, Mia could hardly wait until tonight. She had no choice but to get some painting done this afternoon, and she had no choice but to paint the inside of the Beachcomber after her grandparents returned with the supplies tonight, but after that...

After that, Seth Chandler wouldn't know what hit him. Carmen and Gretel were about to double team him.

SETH WAS totally out of his element amidst the Quentin family. He didn't call the shots. He didn't run the business. He was just a lowly worker—a fact which Mia reminded him of the last time she'd passed him a fresh tray of paint and told him he really ought to take his shirt off while he worked.

Her mixed messages were confusing as hell, but he was definitely liking the sound of the ones she sent him tonight.

They'd all been working—Mia and Noelle, Brock and Seth—to paint the inside of the store ever since Betty and Norman had returned from Tampa with the new paint. Of course, they'd gotten a late start because Betty had nixed the pale blue Mia had ordered and replaced it with bright purple instead.

More lively, Betty insisted.

A better backdrop for the pink flamingo display, added Norman.

After much laughter from Noelle and major teeth grinding from Mia, they'd agreed to paint the store lavender with the help of several healthy doses of white paint. Mia's artistic eye had known just how to balance the colors to produce a unique, pleasing shade.

She'd said something about the color being soothing, but it wasn't having that effect on Seth at all.

The last thing he wanted to do right now was paint, given the hot looks Mia kept tossing his way.

At midnight, however, Noelle had declared the store gorgeous and had sped out of Twin Palms as fast as her moped would take her. Brock laid down his brush and left the store without a word, no doubt a little disappointed the one woman he'd chased in the past five years wouldn't give him the time of day.

But Seth didn't worry too much about Brock right now, not when Mia stood three feet away from him with an expectant look on her face.

And started to peel off her blouse.

A hell of a time for Seth's heart to stop beating, but sure enough, his whole body went silent and still for an endless moment as he watched the unveiling of her golden skin. Although he would have been thrilled to find her naked beneath her clothes, he wasn't the least bit disappointed to discover the red lace bathing suit she'd worn that night on his boat.

"I know what that swimsuit means," he told her once his breath returned.

"You do?" She stared back at him, wide-eyed and not at all innocent as she wriggled her way out of her shorts.

"You're in the market for adventure tonight." High time she'd come to her senses. After they'd sizzled the night away earlier in the week, he hadn't thought she'd be able to deny what they had between them.

But tonight she looked…ready.

"Give that man a prize." She reached for the button on his khakis, his shirt dispensed with hours ago when they'd been painting—on her recommendation. "You're exactly right."

He couldn't think with her hands sliding inside the waist of his pants. The red lace alone was killing him, but her touch was the final blow to his logic.

"Wait." He gripped her wrists and restrained her, gently. He needed to tell her something, needed to make something very clear to her. "Are you ready for more than just one night this time, Mia?"

A moment's hesitation flitted across her features. "I'm ready for more than one night, but maybe not in the way you wanted. I don't have any intention of moving in to be your next live-in love. But I'm ready to see where this takes us."

She sidled closer, a siren in red lace singing him straight to his doom. And damned if he wouldn't be smiling the whole way there.

"So you're committed to the idea of thinking about a commitment?" It was something right?

"Exactly."

The offer might be less than he'd hoped for, but it ranked as more than she'd ever given him. Right now, he wanted her so bad he would take everything she had.

He pulled a spare drop cloth from the arm of an old beach chair. "Then what are we waiting for?"

MIA LET SETH pull her into the warm Florida night air and out onto the deserted Twin Palms beach. The cotton candy, ice cream and fudge vendors were closed up for the night. Even the nighttime volleyball players had gone home, the court lights turned off over the net a hundred yards down the sand.

Mia had no idea what Seth had in mind, but she was game for whatever it might be. Something about him made her feel safe enough to be adventurous, safe enough to let her inner wild woman free. No one but Seth had ever seen the side of her that could stand toe-to-toe with a pirate.

"Where are we going?" she asked, searching the beach for some sign of his destination and growing more curious by the minute about the folded drop cloth he still held in one arm.

They kept walking up the beach, almost to the volleyball net, when Seth tossed the drop cloth onto the sand.

"First we cool off," he pulled her toward the gentle surf. "Then we'll warm up again."

Anticipation moved her bare feet faster. Her skin turned to gooseflesh in the salty night breeze, hungry for the sensual promise behind Seth's words.

The sand grew damp beneath her feet as they neared the ocean's edge. Her toes sank in the squishy grit, but at least the coastline here was happily devoid of any rocks or seaweed. The town of Twin Palms took great pride in their beach and they groomed it accordingly.

"The water's a little cold." She wasn't backing out of the adventure, but growing a bit more cautious as the chilly Gulf nipped at her.

"You have a classic case of cold feet." Seth smiled indulgently, outlined in moonlight and utterly gorgeous.

She could definitely recreate a few pirate fantasies tonight. "Maybe we ought to get straight to the warming up part."

Before she could make a case for the warming up side, Seth scooped her off her feet and charged into the surf with Mia in his arms.

She swore vengeance the whole way in, but maybe she laughed too hard for him to take her seriously.

He'd kicked off his shoes somewhere, but his khakis got soaked as he ran hip deep into the water before falling forward.

Cool water swirled around her, drenching her new bathing suit for the first time. She splashed Seth in the face and chest for revenge. "Don't you know Florida girls don't get in the water until at least May?"

But even as she said it, her body was already adjusting to the temperature as the mild Gulf water wasn't much colder than the night air.

Grinning, he dove under the water without answering to swim silently...somewhere. Mia watched the surface, straining her eyes in the dark to see him.

She never expected to feel him first.

A hand clamped around her thigh beneath the water. Then another hand gripped her other thigh. Gently, the unseen hands tugged her legs apart, her feet skidding easily over the smooth ocean floor.

Unexpected heat churned through her. Seth eased to the surface, still holding her thighs, his dark hair slicked back from his face.

"Do you still want to get out of the water?" His hands skimmed her hips to tug the tiny straps of her bikini bottoms. Water flowed and whirled around her like a caress, moving in reaction to Seth's movements.

"Umm." Thinking became impossible as his fingers slid into her suit to cup the hottest part of her. "I'm going to trust your judgment on that."

"Wise woman." He turned her around in his arms, then hauled her back flush against his chest, pulling them both chest high into the water as he did so.

His hand slid out of her suit to draw the straps down her shoulders. Water lapped at her breasts, swirled around her nipples, and didn't come close to cooling her off.

Seth nipped her shoulder with his teeth, cupped her breast in his hand and teased the nipple between his thumb and forefinger. The relentless roll of waves on the beach matched the persistent tide of anticipation in her veins. She didn't have a chance of warding off the tight coil of longing inside her.

"Seth, I can't wait," she whispered the words, or maybe she shouted them. She couldn't hear anything but waves and water and her own gasping little breaths.

"Don't wait."

She felt his words as much as she heard them, the sounds rumbling through her body.

He dipped one hand into the leg of her swimsuit again, and plied her tender flesh with his fingers.

And with that, she fell, loose-limbed against him, her body gripped with the tiny erotic spasms that Seth seemed to know exactly how to produce.

Delicious languor might have set in, but Seth lifted

her in his arms again, tugging her shoulder straps back into place as he did. The night air chilled her as he carried her back across the beach and stood her by the boardwalk.

Still, even with the saltwater cooling on her skin in the sea breeze, the heat inside her remained banked and ready. She watched in sleepy-lidded fascination as Seth spread the drop cloth beneath the beach's boardwalk, his muscles flexing and water-slick in the moonlight.

His khakis molded to his thighs, outlined clearly exactly how much he already wanted her. Obviously, her body had effectively warmed *him* up already.

And Mia was only too glad to let him take her. She held onto his neck as he picked her up again then laid her on the tarp in the slatted shadow of the planked boardwalk. Seth shoved aside his pants and her bathing suit before he touched her again, but all it took was the slow massage of one finger to stoke the flame inside her again.

Seth being Seth, however, he lowered himself down to her hips to fan his breath across her thighs, to lick the salt from her belly and to kiss her in the most intimate way possible.

She would have spiraled off without him again, but he wouldn't let her, stopping short every time her body quickened with the liquid heat of complete satisfaction. Only when she scratched at his shoulders and pulled him back up her body did he cease his delicious torment to dig a condom out of his discarded pants and bury himself deeply inside her.

Mia cried out at the mixture of fulfillment and the

new hunger for more. He felt so good, so right inside her, on top of her, all around her.

How could she have walked away from a night like this? How would she ever walk away from *him?*

Unwilling to think about how much he expected from her, let alone how much she wanted to give him, Mia let her thoughts skitter to the way the sand molded against her back through the tarp, the way the drying ocean water left salty crystals on her legs, anything but the intense pleasure of Seth between her thighs. If she thought too much about the languid slide of his movements one minute, or the urgent press of his body the next, she'd be hurtling over the edge, lost in waves of ecstasy.

"Mia," Seth growled the word into her hair, anchoring her to him. "I want you with me now."

She braved a glance up at him, dark and shadowed in their makeshift hideaway. The planes of his face seemed bold, striking, stark except for the softness of his full lips. His chest loomed, broad and perfect and begging for her touch.

"I come apart too fast if I think about it too much," she confided, her fingers already eating up his chest, absorbing the soft bristle of hair. The smooth strength of muscle.

"Honey, you can let yourself go again and again and again if you're capable. Most women would kill for that ability."

She propped herself up on her elbows to be closer to him. "I thought I would, um, make you come with me if I lose it too fast."

He thought for a minute, then rolled onto his back,

allowing her to sit on top of him. "Not this way you won't. Maybe." He clamped his hands around her waist to guide her where he wanted her to go.

And gave her several ideas of her own in the process.

Two orgasms later, he came right with her, losing himself in her as thoroughly as she seemed to drown in him. His groan echoed under the boardwalk, alerting anyone within a few hundred yards that they were under there. And having a really good time.

Mia hardly minded the sandy, gritty walk back to the boathouse. She had just learned a few things about her adventurous self.

Not the least of which was that she was multi-orgasmic.

It had been a very good night.

SETH LAY in Mia's bed at dawn the next morning, listening to her deep even breathing as he studied the relaxed lines of her face in sleep.

She was amazing. Never had he met a woman so in tune with her own wants, so sensually aware of herself that she could fly apart with a few well-placed touches. Yet in the course of one night, she'd learned to hold back too, and to feel the effect of saving up all the sexual energy for one bigger, bed-rattling release.

She'd thanked him as she looked up at him with sated eyes, had declared him to be a sex god and too good to be true. How could he not fall for a woman like that?

And it was feeling frighteningly close to a "falling'' sensation. He'd been on more even footing with the women he'd lived with—women who knew what he'd expected of them and who had certain expectations of him in return.

Mia expected nothing. She wanted the here and now and no talk of tomorrows because she couldn't commit to anything beyond today.

But damn it, he needed to offer her something. If he couldn't provide for her with a house or by paying the bills, he had to find something else he could give her to let her know that he wasn't going anywhere.

Then he remembered how many hours she'd been putting into the store renovations and inspiration struck. Suddenly, he knew exactly where to start.

12

MIA TOLD HERSELF she didn't mind waking up alone.

In fact, she told herself several times as she wound her hair into a ponytail and pulled on a yellow tank top. Tucking her shirt into a pair of camouflage print shorts, Mia launched into a mental litany of reasons she was happy about Seth giving her a little space.

Number one, she didn't have abandonment issues. No siree. Just because a girl had a mother with wandering feet who didn't have enough time to raise a daughter did *not* mean she would run scared from relationships for the rest of her life.

Number two, if anything, she had worried about Seth trying to entice her to give up her artistic leanings and to move in with him in Tampa.

Obviously, she didn't have to worry about that happening if he couldn't even be bothered to stick around when she woke up in the morning. Especially after a night of incredible sex that would have convinced most couples they were somehow celestially destined to be together.

By the time she stomped across the sandy driveway between her boathouse and the Beachcomber, Mia couldn't deny she was fairly upset. What if she'd wanted to repay Seth this morning for all those sexual favors he'd given her last night?

Clearly, the man had missed a fabulous opportunity.

She was so busy envisioning scenarios of what might have happened this morning if Seth hadn't left, that she didn't even see who was headed her way until she almost tripped over him.

"Whoa!" Frankie Bollino, the manager of the marina next door and the only acceptable bachelor for Mia according to Grandpa, steadied Mia's shoulders before she pitched face first into the sand. "Sorry, Mia. I was backing up to see if the sign for the shop was still crooked. What do you think?"

Mia eyed the Beachcomber sign critically. It had been sliding down at an angle for months. Now it perched high over the front door, perfectly level.

"It looks great, Frankie. Thanks."

"I saw it was pretty busy over here this morning so I thought I'd give 'em a hand." Frankie shrugged as he shoved his hammer into a loop on his pants. "You know how men are—we tend to congregate around tools."

Honestly, she had no clue how men were. "Is Seth still here?"

"I think he's putting together some shelves inside, but I've gotta get back to the marina."

Mia nodded, not sure if she felt grateful for Seth's help or a little resentful that he would take over the renovations without so much as consulting her.

A nice person would simply be grateful, right? But

damn it, how did he know what she wanted done on the store?

Mia barreled into the shop, ready to go to the mat to make sure the updated store looked exactly like she wanted it to. She'd done enough compromising yesterday when she gave in on the purple paint, even though she had to admit, the lavender they'd ended up with was perfect.

The sight that greeted her eyes definitely wasn't what she'd expected. She'd been ready for Seth to be hanging shelves in all the wrong places. She wasn't prepared to see Seth working side by side with Noelle, Brock and Mia's grandparents.

For once, her grandparents weren't bickering with Noelle. And for once, everyone seemed to be following her renovation plan instead of creating their own visions of what they thought the Beachcomber should look like.

Hadn't she always needed to play peacemaker in her family, to run interference when trouble brewed—which in the Quentins' case was almost every day?

Her grandmother smiled from her perch on a folding chair along one side of the room while Brock and Seth struggled to fit together hardwood for the new flooring on the other. Seth gave her a sexy grin that was pretty damn potent even with his shirt still on, then went back to concentrating on the floor.

"We tried to tell your pirate he didn't have to help us, but he refused to listen," Betty grumbled between bites of the oversize danish sold by the coffee shop up the street.

"He's damn stubborn," Norman agreed, though without any real venom.

Dear God. Her grandparents were beginning to like Seth. How was she going to keep him at arm's length if he'd even managed to win *them* over?

She didn't stand a chance against pirate charm. She'd be live-in love number six in no time at this rate. And she'd get dumped in the end somehow too, just like all of Seth's other mysterious lovers.

And even though she definitely did *not* have abandonment issues, Mia was just a little afraid that was going to hurt a bit more than she could bear.

NOELLE SENSED Mia's inner turmoil clear across the store. Only a fellow Quentin could fully appreciate how unnerving it would be to see the guy you liked grudgingly accepted into the family fold. Honestly, how could Norman's taste run parallel to any woman in the world save Betty's?

Very bizarre.

But whether or not the morning's incident would seem disturbing to anyone else was irrelevant. Right now, Mia looked like she was either going to cry, throw something or perhaps explode into screaming all the frustrated thoughts she'd been carrying around in her very polite Mia brain for the past decade.

"Umm, Brock?" Noelle couldn't help it that she called on the silent, sexy star of all of her fantasies for a little assistance, could she? "Would you mind helping me entertain my parents for a while this morning? I think Mia wants to work on a secret project with Seth. Right, Mia?"

Mia nodded, her movements fast and jerky. "Right."

Brock slowly unfolded himself from his spot on the floor. Noelle's mouth went dry, as it seemed to every time she looked at the man. There was something about those fantastically broad shoulders that made a woman think there wasn't any burden this guy couldn't bear. Sick thinking for an independent woman fast approaching forty, right? She didn't need any help with her burdens thank you very much.

She just liked to look.

"Sure." Brock headed for the front door. "Norman, you want to take the boat out for a couple of hours and see how the fishing looks?"

Her father ditched his danish like a kid called to recess. "Great day for fishing."

Traitor. How could her father have been swayed to Brock's side in so short a time? Didn't he worry about his only daughter at all anymore? And what about the so-called ulcer of his?

Thanks to her father's defection, not only had Brock avoided spending the day with *her,* he had also conveniently stuck her with her mother. For a couple of *hours* no less.

And Noelle wasn't even going to consider the fact that her folks liked Brock as much as they liked Seth. That didn't matter one iota since she was in no way, shape or form ever going to get involved with Brock Chandler.

Noelle watched Brock's departing broad shoulders and her father's more slight form as they headed out the door. Was it her imagination, or did Norman walk a little taller as he left on his fishing quest, free from the tourist shop for a few hours?

"Well I guess that leaves you and me." Betty Quentin looked at her daughter with a challenge in her eyes and folded her arms across the peacock-blue blouse she wore. "There's no one left for you to foist me on."

No time like the present to mend familial fences, right? Part of her had always wondered if healing the rift with her mother would somehow smooth her relationship with her daughter as well.

"And whatever gave you the impression I don't delight in your company?" She handed Betty her blue leather coin purse. "We don't need those men to take Twin Palms by storm."

Noelle braced herself for a maternal set-down. But her mother upped the ante by snatching purse out of her hand and marching toward the door.

"Take the town by storm. What are we going to do, order bagels instead of sandwiches for lunch? Or maybe we can really go crazy and get a pedicure at the Cut 'n Curl?"

Treading lightly on this semifun mood of her mother's, Noelle picked up her purse and followed after her.

"Was that a joke, mother?"

"Certainly not. You've always said I have no sense of humor." Betty had already hit the driveway when she turned to stare back up at Noelle on the store's front steps. "Now, don't forget the helmets, dear. I'm not taking anything by storm unless I get to try out the moped."

"Mom, you can't be serious."

"I'm perfectly serious. It's your father who has the delicate constitution, not me." She frowned so hard she added wrinkles to her tanned skin in every direction. "I hope your young man knows that about Norman."

Noelle led the way to the garage, incapable of being annoyed about the "your young man" comment, not when her mother looked genuinely worried.

She passed her mother a helmet and shoved her own on her head. "Brock doesn't strike me as the kind of guy who will do anything too crazy out on the water. If he boats as slow as he walks, our only concern will be whether or not Daddy makes it back tonight or tomorrow morning." Which brought to mind questions of how Brock did other things...such as make love? Would it be as slow, as intense, as he'd promised?

Noelle hadn't slept a wink since he'd spelled out exactly how it would be between them.

"You're right." Betty looked reassured, her wrinkles reassembling into the softer, gentler pattern of her smile as she strapped on the helmet. "Why don't you let me do the driving sweetie and I'll show you where you got all your adventurous genes from?"

SETH STARTED to get suspicious right about the time Noelle cleared house. Even Mia's grandmother agreed to vacate the store—something Seth had quickly realized she rarely did—to leave Seth and Mia alone. Brock had obviously done a hell of a job selling Mia's grandparents on Seth.

He set his hammer down on the floor, mentally making a note of how many more floorboards he needed to complete the current row he was laying down. Rising to his feet, he got a better look at Mia—her stiff posture, her scowling eyebrows, the general steam hissing from her ears.

"What's the matter?"

"You're looking awfully comfortable in Twin Palms, Seth." Mia idly cleaned up the leftover papers and coffee cups from the takeout breakfast on a small folding table. "And you're looking pretty at ease with my family, too."

He'd been feeling pretty good about that himself, actually. "Your grandparents aren't as cantankerous as they pretend. I think they're just used to scaring off your boyfriends."

Mia nodded, her dark hair sweeping up and down over her shoulders. "Yes, I guess so. They like to protect me from men who won't be good for me."

Go Norman. Seth could appreciate a man looking out for his family. He'd gladly keelhaul any loser who didn't treat his sister right. "Makes sense."

"Then why don't you tell me what you think you're accomplishing by working your way into my family's hearts?" Mia pinned him with an uncanny gaze, her green cat eyes seeing right through him. "I told you how much my grandfather worries about me and the guys I date."

"But he likes me."

Mia looked at him like he'd sprouted an extra head. Or like he'd lost half his brain cells. "How much is he going to like you when he realizes your ceiling for a relationship is the live-in stage?''

Mia dumped the empty danish box into the trashcan with a flourish.

Damn. Seth felt the slam all the way to his guilty conscience. ''Who says I have a ceiling?''

She shook her head, her smile slow and sad. ''Look, it's fine with me. For now. I'm waist-deep in family commitments and financial obligations anyway. I just don't want to flaunt such a temporary relationship under my grandfather's nose and send the poor guy running back to the hospital with his ulcer.''

Shit. This morning was not going at all like he'd anticipated. He'd come down to the store to work on the floor to show Mia his level of commitment, not push her farther away. How come the more he tried to win this woman, the more ground he seemed to lose?

''You can't back out on me already.'' Last night wasn't something they could just walk away from. At least, he sure as hell couldn't.

''I'm not backing out.'' She drifted closer, a hint of a smile warming her face, giving him hope. ''I just don't want you to engage my grandparents' hearts, then sail off into the sunset once things between us aren't all you'd imagined. It might be better if—''

He made the time-out sign with his hands. ''Wait a minute. That's never been the case with me, Mia. I've never given up on a relationship.''

''Don't tell me all your girlfriends left you.'' She

picked up a small silver ring with dozens of paint sample cards hanging off of it and fanned out the colors.

Was there any good way to answer this question? "Hard to believe considering I'm a pretty good guy, right?"

"Did you force out the other party with slow death of affection or something?" She ran a finger over all the colors, lingering on each one.

"No." Had he? "Maybe. I don't know, Mia."

She mirrored the time-out gesture he'd made earlier. "It doesn't matter. I want to be with you, in spite of what might have happened in the past. All I'm saying is that I wish you'd be careful flexing the Chandler charm around my grandparents."

"Got it. No winking at Betty." He drew her closer, eager for a feel of her bare shoulders, her golden, tanned skin. "What about your mother?"

"You can try to charm her all you want." She slid her arms around his waist, insinuated herself up against him. "She seems to be developing a thick skin for you Chandler men."

Her hands wandered up and down his back, at once relaxing him and teasing him, too. Last night, her hands hadn't been nearly so gentle on his back when they'd been rolling around at the beach.

"My money's still on Brock," Seth offered, hoping to distract himself before he dragged Mia back to the boathouse. "He's got a lot of patience and I've never seen him like this about another woman."

"Really?" Mia looked up at him with undisguised

longing for all of two seconds before she nodded quickly and stepped out of his arms.

"What?" He couldn't quite read her expression.

"I'm sure Brock is a great guy. It's just that my mother's been through some major man crises and I hate to see her get hurt."

Seth had the feeling she had more on her mind than what she was saying, but he had his plate full just trying to figure out where he stood with her let alone trying to determine how Brock was faring. "I'll warn my uncle to be on his best behavior."

She nodded, satisfied. "You think we ought to finish up the floor before everyone comes back?"

He'd lost this round, big time.

Nodding, he reached for the next floorboard to get back to work. His effort to offer Mia something of himself had backfired in ways he had never anticipated. Now, he needed to make up for lost ground and somehow show her he was about more than a live-in relationship.

Of course, it could be a challenge to do that considering Seth had no idea what he *could* offer her outside of free rent and a promise to always be there for her. Besides, what if he sucked at long-term commitments as much as his old man had? As much as his brother, Jesse, still did.

The notion might have given him pause if he wasn't so hell-bent determined to win Mia no matter what it took.

MIA HAD TO ADMIT she and Seth could lay down floorboards like professionals. And she didn't need to remember last night to know they were a spectacular match in bed. No, all she had to do was take her pulse when Seth moved within two feet of her.

They made a great team.

But something about his intense gaze, his extreme focus—sometimes on the new hardwood floor, sometimes on her—made her feel like he was strategizing his next move more than he was enjoying their time together.

Did that sound hypersensitive? Probably. But Mia had learned to follow her instincts where people were concerned, and she caught a competitive vibe from Seth that struck her as both incredibly sexy and a little daunting, too.

She didn't want to think of herself as the prize in the corporate shark's next big investment scheme. Did he somehow weigh her price in floorboards and danishes? And would he even still be interested in her once the thrill of the chase had ended?

Splitting up with Seth would be painful no matter what. Of course, it would be even worse if Brock and Noelle got together. Then she and Seth would be stuck seeing each other, being polite, remaining part of one another's lives.

They had just finished securing the last stretch of new baseboard when the door to the store flung wide open, allowing a gust of salty sea air to drift inside and setting off the electronic bell attached to the entrance.

"I'm sorry, we're closed—" Mia began before she saw the newcomer's vaguely familiar smile.

Topping six foot by at least an inch or two, the

stranger's dark hair, brown eyes and wicked grin conspired to remind her of someone.

"Hey, Seth," the stranger started, dropping a backpack on the floor of the store and crossing the new hardwood in three strides. "Next time you leave town, you damn well better turn your cell phone on."

From the threatening tone of the man's voice, Mia half expected him to take a swing at Seth. Instead the two men clamped each other in a partial bear hug that involved much beating on one another's backs.

"I'm only using the tricks you taught me, you dog." Seth released the man, and turned to Mia. "This is my brother, Jesse. Jesse, this is Mia Quentin."

No wonder he looked familiar. He had all of Seth's good looks without the steely intensity. Now that the two stood side by side, she could see the resemblance immediately, though Seth stood maybe half an inch taller than his brother. Judging by Jesse's ready smile and warm gaze, however, Mia thought he seemed much more ready to give himself over to fun than Seth.

Jesse approached her, both hands out as if to envelop her in a bear hug, too.

Mia held out one hand in defense, ready to limit their first hello to a handshake.

Right about the same time Seth barked, "She's also mine."

Jesse's pout was dramatic but good-natured. "I go to all the trouble of driving your boat up here only to find you've stolen the prettiest girl in Twin

Palms." He shook Mia's hand and winked. "A pleasure to meet you, Mia."

"Likewise." She stepped out of the way and began repacking the toolbox. Her conversation with Seth—not that she'd been eager to revisit the nature of their relationship anyway—would have to wait until later. "Feel free to go visit, you guys. There's lots of good food at the beach if you're ready for lunch."

Jesse bent to help her, tossing pliers and nails into place. "I already scoped out the gyros. Lunch is on me, Mia, and I need a woman's advice more than I need to catch up with the banker anyway."

"The banker?" She let Jesse move the toolbox aside, intrigued by his nickname for Seth.

Jesse rolled his eyes while Seth cuffed him in the arm. Mia wondered if she and her mother would get along better if they allowed themselves occasional punches.

"Yeah, the banker. Seth is pretty much made of money, you know."

"Then by all means, let's make him buy lunch." How could she resist Jesse's request for a woman's opinion? Especially when she might learn more interesting things about Seth while she was at it.

An hour later, they sipped cold beers under a red and white striped umbrella table in front of a gyro stand called Constantine's. Mia had learned all sorts of interesting things about Seth over lunch, including that he'd turned into the family provider when his father walked out on a wife and three kids.

No wonder the guy was commitment shy—he'd

obviously been burdened with enough responsibility in his life.

"So out with it, Jesse." Seth clanked his bottle against his brother's, making Jesse's brew bubble all the way up the neck and forcing him to take a long swig. "You didn't just come up here to return my boat that I really didn't need."

Jesse chugged a few more gulps to settle the bubbles and smacked his lips. "Nope. I'm hiding out from Kyra, if you must know."

"Kyra?"

Seth turned to Mia to fill in. "That's his sort of business partner. She's an old friend of the family's."

Jesse snorted, but he also seemed to gauge Seth's reaction carefully, as if he put stock in his older brother's advice. "Some friend."

"Kyra's as loyal as they come," Seth argued.

Mia could hear the affection, the ready defensiveness in his voice. A hint of jealousy niggled at the back of her mind, but she squashed it firmly.

Jesse shook his head. "You wouldn't believe what she's doing to me. She dressed up as a lady pirate for Gasparilla and kidnapped me at knifepoint."

Seth nearly spewed his beer at that one.

Even not knowing this Kyra person, Mia had to admit she enjoyed the vision of a bold-as-brass woman taking the obvious bad-boy Jesse to be her prisoner. Besides, from Mia's point of view, Kyra wasn't sounding all that intimidating.

While Seth continued to alternately choke on his beer and laugh, Jesse looked to Mia for help. "She's still following me, Mia. I don't know how to get it through to her that I can't be with her *that* way."

Mia might have asked a few more questions to get a handle on the situation, pleased to worry about someone else's love life rather than her own. It looked like both Chandler brothers had commitment problems, a family trait that hurt Mia more than it should. But before she could say a word, Seth intervened.

"Why not, Jesse? You've been with half the other women in St. Petersburg."

Jesse slammed his empty beer bottle down on the table. "She's my best frigging friend!"

He stalked away from the table and fumed his way down the beach while she and Seth stared helplessly at one another.

"I'd better go talk to him," Seth said finally, a lifetime of being responsible for his family evident in his concerned expression.

Mia nodded and watched him walk away, enjoying the view and wondering what kind of guidance Seth would give his brother regarding love.

Would he suggest Jesse pursue Kyra with the same full-tilt determination Seth seemed to pursue *her?* No. Seth in older brother mode would operate a little differently. He'd offer up something practical and reasonable, no doubt.

But no matter how certain she was Seth would roll out some wise, sound logic for his brother, she couldn't help hoping he would ignore all that good judgment and common sense when it came to her.

13

MIA STOOD AT her portable easel on the beach and checked the warm golden light of sunset over the Gulf before dipping her brush into the orange paint again. She worked quickly, frantic to capture the soft glow of color before it faded into the horizon.

Desperate to forget today's news regarding her family's loan.

She would have enjoyed a few minutes with Seth today. Not that she would ever burden him with her financial woes, but she could have used a hug, a touch. One of his great smiles that made her insides warm and liquid.

But he'd been on the phone with business associates all day and had only been down to the beach once—to say he'd join her for sunset. As the sun dipped farther and farther down in the sky, Mia had to wonder if Seth's work often overshadowed his life.

She had no idea what time it was or how many minutes had passed in the smooth stroking of paint on canvas when her mother joined her. Noelle dropped into the sand at Mia's feet to watch nature's display.

"You're painting like a woman possessed," Noelle observed, lying on her side and propping her head on a black leather backpack. "Is this a really great sunset or something?"

Mia examined the light again and mixed in a bit of yellow just over her waves. "No. But it might very well be the last good sunset we have before my show next weekend."

And Mia planned to have enough paintings available at the show to sell to all of Tampa. God knew, she needed the money now more than ever. Thankfully, she'd been productive lately, perhaps because her senses had been inspired at every turn by a certain overworked pirate.

"It's just that you look a bit…tense…for a woman painting such a serene subject." Her mother drew her own pictures in the sand, not that Mia was paying any attention to her. Noelle had always been incredibly difficult to ignore.

Especially when the sand graphics flicked grit onto Mia's calves.

Mia slapped paint on the canvas with a bit more force than necessary. "Actually Mom, I'm more than tense. And while I paint this serene subject for an art show that no one's going to attend, I'm actually thinking about how devastated Grammie and Grandpa are going to be when the bank puts up a big 'Foreclosed' sign next week."

"Please say you're joking." Her mother sat up, squashing her sand drawings to give Mia her full attention.

"Only partially." Tears of frustration burned the backs of her eyeballs, not that she would ever shed them in front of Noelle. "The woman I met with last week called me to say she can't do anything to help us after all. Because the economy is tightening up, the bank is less flexible with delinquent loans. We're not getting foreclosed on yet, but we have been officially turned over to a collection agency and our banknote is up for grabs if another business wanted to purchase it.'' The sense of failure weighed heavily on Mia's shoulders. Too bad she didn't have the business acumen of Seth the corporate shark. Maybe she would have been able to circumvent this mess. "Why didn't I try harder to get Grammie and Grandpa to update the store years ago?"

"You can't let yourself think like that." Her mother stood, brushing sand off her tanned legs. "Your grandparents are loving, wonderful people but they are also colossally stubborn when it comes to their business. I think it took the slow slide into red ink to make them really start to listen to you."

Mia added red and purple to her picture in a painting frenzy, seized with the desire to do something right today, to create beauty on canvas even if she'd created a big mess with real life.

The tears she'd been swallowing back all day made a new push forward when her mother laid a comforting hand on her back. She'd been in need of comfort—wishing Seth could just hold her—for the past eight hours. But Noelle's surprising sensitivity about the Beachcomber took her by surprise.

"I can help," Noelle offered, tucking a strand of Mia's unbound hair behind one ear.

Mia shook her head. She was grateful for the offer but wanted to shoulder the burden of the Beachcomber herself. It was a point of pride, a physical manifestation of the bond she'd always shared with her grandparents.

"Thanks, Mom, but you've already given up too much of your time for the business this year. I don't know how you find time to write your lessons and grade your papers too, but I owe you a huge thank you for helping us out this year."

"I still don't even have the damn register figured out. How much help could I have been?" Noelle rolled her eyes. "I want to buy the banknote and put an end to the foreclosure worries, Mia. I can drive into Tampa tomorrow and take care of it."

Mia's brush stopped moving across the canvas. She blinked to clear her brain of the wrong impression she'd just received from her mother.

"I'm sorry. I must have been lost in an artistic vision for a moment. Did you just say *you* were going to purchase a twelve thousand dollar banknote?"

Noelle offered a crooked smile, her hand slipping from Mia's back to retrieve her backpack from the beach. "Yes. And now that I think on it, I believe I can fund an account at another bank directly from my bank so I won't even need to take the day off." She hitched her backpack onto her shoulder, as if ready to flee.

And with damn good reason.

Anger whipped through Mia, a refreshing tide of red-hot emotion that felt infinitely better than the fear and worry that had bitten at her all day. Ever since she'd met Seth she seemed incapable of tucking her emotions neatly away. Lately, she'd had no choice but to express her feelings and she sure needed to now.

She jammed her palette into a wooden tray on the front of the easel and stuffed the paintbrush in there alongside it before turning on her mother.

"I don't mean to sound ungrateful." She took deep breaths to will away the hurt she felt at her mother's lack of faith in her. "But I'm a bit surprised you could have saved that much money since you came back to Twin Palms. For that matter, if you have twelve thousand dollars to your name, why have you chosen to live in a hotel for the past three years and give everyone the impression you're making this stay as temporary as possible? Again." The words came out harsher than she'd intended, but her real feelings poured out in a tide of hurt.

Noelle opened her mouth to say something but Mia had no intention of letting her mother get a word in edgewise.

"But I do know that there's no way you are going to ride into this family now, after all these years, and throw some money around to fix the wounds between us."

"That is so unfair of you—"

"And that's pretty unfair of you to roll out your new checkbook and rob me of my chance to make this right." Mia lifted her canvas off the easel and collapsed the wooden stand with one hand. "I know I haven't given you much reason to have faith in me or my work, Mom. But I don't need the money because I'm making my own plans to pay off the debt with my show this weekend. Thanks anyway."

As she started to walk away, Mia could hear her mother shouting something about stubbornness not paying the bills and that she only wanted to help.

That was just the damn problem. Everybody wanted to help her. What she needed was for somebody to believe in her.

Her grandparents wanted to impose their vision of the Beachcomber on the store no matter how many years it hadn't worked. Seth wanted to provide for her and take over her store renovations so she didn't have to get her fingernails dirty or work too hard. His need to take over, while generous, just demonstrated that he didn't really want a committed, sharing partnership.

Now, her mother's offer to buy their way out of the mess only clarified her lack of faith in Mia, too. Luckily, Mia had enough faith in herself—and her art—for all of them.

At least she hoped she did.

Trudging up the beach toward the boathouse with all her gear in tow, she nearly plowed right over Seth.

"Hey gorgeous, need help?" He lifted her painting out of her arms. "You okay?"

As long as she didn't cry in front of him, she could afford a few moments to soak up his strength, to sink in his arms, couldn't she?

Unable to answer for fear of setting free the tears begging to be released, Mia settled for an emphatic shake of her head.

His arms were around her in a heartbeat, soothing her hellish day and comforting her on a soul-deep level. It frightened her a little to realize how connected she felt to this man, how much his touch meant to her right now.

The realization that the fate of her grandparents' store rested on her shoulders staggered her enough. And since her fight with Noelle, she had also somehow tacked on the additional burden of proving herself as an artist and a savvy businessperson to her whole family.

She definitely couldn't afford to question her scary new feelings for a man who'd come to mean too much to her, too soon.

NOELLE SLAMMED down the phone in the hotel room that had served as her home for nearly three years. Two hours after her showdown with Mia and she was still furious. Hurt.

But she'd taken the necessary steps to start feeling better. Since Mia was so adamantly opposed to her mother's money, Noelle would use it to seize her own dream. She'd just made a verbal agreement to purchase the property on the other side of the marina, effectively tying herself to Twin Palms for the first time in over twenty years.

On her own terms.

Still wound up on the adrenaline generated by her argument with Mia, Noelle charged through her room to the closet, flinging off her clothes in her wake.

Tonight, she would celebrate her own life for a change. Sure she'd been hopelessly selfish while Mia had been growing up. But she had made every effort to be a team player the past few years and now she just needed to face the fact that she would never be accepted as a full-fledged Quentin again.

Her old relationship with her mother seemed positively peachy compared to the fast collapse of her bond with Mia.

Noelle pulled out one outfit after another from the closet, determined to find something wild and dangerous from her former life in the depths of her wardrobe. She wanted something slinky. Something jaw-dropping. Something suited to her rebel roots.

Her fingers paused over an ancient silver lace dress. The skirt skimmed her thighs at an alarming height while the plunging neckline and cap sleeves showed off plenty of cleavage. All she needed were her thigh high black leather boots and her motorcycle jacket to make her look as dangerous outside as she felt on the inside. Of course, she wouldn't exactly be a pistol-packing mama while seated astride her moped instead of a Harley.

But a woman had to work with what she had at hand.

Sliding into the slim lace dress, Noelle thanked her Stairmaster and marginal sense of self-discipline that she still managed to squeeze herself into the garment. But it's not like she needed to go out dancing in the dress, after all.

A day like this deserved to be capped off in style, and Noelle couldn't think of any more fitting way to end it than in Brock Chandler's bed.

BROCK WONDERED if he'd ever get to bed at this rate. He'd been listening to his nephews rant over one woman concern after another for the last hour since dinner. Didn't they know he had his own damn problems to worry about? Noelle's tougher-than-leather facade made dealing with Mia or Jesse's girlfriend Kyra seem like child's play.

"You're telling me they're behind in their mortgage payments and that's why Mia is working on that damn store twenty-four hours a day?" Seth glared at his uncle from his perch on the bow rail of Brock's fishing boat.

"Norman said they would have hit foreclosure long ago if it hadn't been for Mia putting off the bank." He related the same information for the third time, knowing it had probably been a mistake to share financial woes with Seth Chandler, Corporate Wunderkind. "But I'm sure Mia has a plan. I really don't think it's any of our business."

Jesse propped his boots up on the rail next to his brother and leaned back in his aluminum folding chair. "Kyra would kill me if I got in between her and her accounting ledger. That's why I'm the silent partner."

Seth nudged Jesse's feet off the rail, sending his boots to the planked deck with a thud. "That's because Kyra watched firsthand while you blew off all your accounting classes to chase girls in college."

"Hey, I've got my degree." Jesse balled up a paper napkin left over from their takeout pizza dinner and threw it square in Seth's face.

Brock considered collaring them both and dumping them overboard for a late-night swim, but opted to suggest they retire to Seth's boat instead. Sometimes it sucked being a patient man when being impulsive would be a hell of a lot more fun.

"I'll never sleep knowing Mia might be in trouble with the bank." Seth headed for the dock, picking up his overnight bag on the way. "I might take Jesse back to Tampa tonight and stop in at Gulf Coast to see how bad things are for the Beachcomber."

Bad, bad idea kid. "Why don't you just try talking to her instead?" Had Brock been this thickheaded at thirty? No wonder he was still single.

"She had a fight with her mom tonight and she's pretty upset." Seth shook his head, steely determination in his eyes. "I'm not going to bring this up when she's already reeling from a tough day."

Brock might have worked harder to dissuade him, but the mention of Noelle distracted him. Was she upset tonight, too?

Seth was already stalking down the dock toward his own boat when Jesse clapped Brock on the shoulder. "I'll try and talk him out of it," he confided. "For all the good it will do. Thanks for dinner."

Brock cuffed his younger nephew in the chest. "You worry about your own neck, Jess. I've never seen Kyra go gunning for any man before, so I have the feeling she means business."

Jesse rubbed his throat protectively. "You won't see a noose around this neck any time soon."

Brock waved them off and watched Seth steer his boat out of the marina. Toward Tampa and toward trouble, no doubt.

He half wondered if he ought to follow his nephew into the calm Gulf waters for the short southern cruise. Was he being as thickheaded as Seth by staying in Twin Palms when Noelle so obviously wanted him to go?

The warm night air swirled around him on the deck, the whine of a faraway boat mingling with the constant lap of waves against the fiberglass hull. Maybe later this week he'd pull out of the marina and leave Noelle alone.

The drone of the boat engine hummed closer, fracturing his thoughts and subtly transforming in his mind until it began to sound more like a...moped?

Brock turned from his ocean view to look back toward the shore. And there, shooting down the marina's planked boardwalk in a highly illegal maneuver was Noelle. Only this Noelle wasn't the worried, single mother he'd kissed in the Beachcomber storeroom. No, this Noelle wore leather stiletto boots up to her thighs and sported a tiny, silvery dress that *still* didn't meet the tops of those boots.

Lust tugged at him with more force than the fiercest big game fish he'd ever wrestled. Hell, he'd gladly allow her to pull him overboard with *that* outfit as the lure.

The leather biker jacket and black chauffeur's hat on her head didn't exactly diminish the sexy effect of her outfit. Brock's mouth watered, blood boiled and whole body tensed just looking at her.

He wandered over to the boat rail for a closer inspection as she slowed the moped to a stop and swung one leg over the seat. Damn the angle of his view from higher up—he missed out on any panty flashing that might have taken place.

"Nice night for a ride." He leaned over the rail to ogle her openly, unable to remove his gaze from the leather and lace, sinful and sexy vision she made. Good God, the woman was dangerous.

"Nice night to go after what you want in life," she shot back, pausing at the edge of the dock to peer up at him. "Can I come aboard?"

Brock's slow nod was the best response he could currently manage.

He'd apparently just swallowed his damn tongue.

EVEN THOUGH Brock's nod wasn't exactly brimming with enthusiasm, Noelle accepted it as an invitation. No way would she turn back now, not after the day she'd had.

Hopping from dock to boat deck provided a bit of challenge in her narrow cut dress, but Noelle somehow managed the crossing without bursting a seam. She smoothed her fingers over the silver lace dress as if to absorb a little of its come hither attitude in the wake of Brock's lukewarm greeting.

Taking a deep breath she steeled herself for the walk to the bow to close the distance between them, but before she could march her feet forward, he materialized in front of her.

Strong, solid and sexy as hell, Brock looked better in his faded gray T-shirt sporting a blue marlin than any of the thick-necked weightlifters who populated the Twin Palms beach every day of the week.

And now that he loomed this close, Noelle could see by the heat in his gaze that he was anything but lukewarm. He watched her like the experienced fisherman tests his catch, giving her a little line to see what she would do with the extra room to flee.

"I wasn't expecting you." He perused her up and down, his dark eyes taking a slow cruise over every leather-and-lace clad inch. "You look…like you're spoiling for trouble."

"Is that a good thing?"

A smile kicked up one side of his lips. "It is if you're me. But if I were you I'd definitely be worried about getting arrested on the ride home. Or causing massive traffic accidents at the very least."

Pleasure soothed her nerves, floated through her veins, and made everything inside her feel settled and reckless at the same time.

She longed to stroke her hands all over him, but some annoyingly old-fashioned part of her wanted him to touch her first. So she toyed with the zipper on her jacket and rocked back and forth on sky-high heels that made her almost as tall as Brock.

She locked gazes with him and let her words do her seducing for her.

"Then I guess it's a good thing I'm not going home."

Brock took a deep breath and exhaled it out with a noisy puff. "You're fully armed tonight, aren't you?"

"It's an all-out assault, Brock. Watch out." She just hoped it would start working. Soon.

He opened his mouth as if he was ready to say something, then his eyes tripped their way down her body again. He cursed, closed his eyes, and started again. "Damn it, Noelle, but that dress is distracting.

It's killing me not to touch you right now, but before I forget my own name tonight, I'd like to at least know what brought you here, because it sure as hell wasn't anything I did.''

"Does it matter?" She didn't want to think about her fight with Mia or the fact that her daughter would never accept her as more than a pseudosister in her life.

"A little, it matters." His hands reached for her, stopped, then locked firmly behind his neck as if imprisoning one another. "I can't help but wonder if this is a one time gift from the gods or if I might find you on my doorstep—or gangplank, as it were— again someday."

She definitely liked thinking of herself as a gift from the gods. Her mood improved along with her eagerness to get her hands all over this man. She walked away from him toward the middle of the boat in search of the cabin area. "I'm buying the beach-front property."

"You're kidding." He released his fingers and followed her.

"Mia doesn't want my money and made it very clear she doesn't want my help either." Noelle blinked quickly, refusing to let her eyes burn. "As of tonight, I'm living my life for me." She started down the short set of steps to the cabin area in the hull of the boat. "On my terms."

When she hit the bottom step, she faced three closed doors. Brock stopped just behind her and gently steered her shoulders to the door in the middle. His touch burned right through her, melting her insides and making her want to sink back into him.

"I know that had to hurt like hell, Noelle. But I'm not sorry you made the right decision."

Breathless from her own want, she turned the brass handle and nudged the door open. Brock's bedroom came into view, a small cabin dominated by a huge bed and all but wallpapered in maps. Maps of islands, maps of the world, navigational maps, and a lone, round globe of the earth in a light oak stand at the foot of his bed.

She wondered idly if Brock Chandler possessed the same wandering feet she'd been born with.

Of course, she didn't wonder for long because his hands slipped around her shoulders to peel her jacket down her arms. Cool air drifted over her partially bared skin, followed in quick succession by the searing heat of his gaze.

"Your life on your terms, Noelle," his voice rasped in her ear, the gruff edginess making her skin tingle and tighten. "You're not going to regret it."

The door fell shut behind them, casting them in shadows from the dim light of two high portholes. The wavery reflection of the water spilled across the navy blue bedspread, providing a shifting, quicksilver pattern.

She turned toward him, ready to be in his arms, a part of him. But he wasn't there where she'd expected him. He was kneeling over her feet.

"What are you doing?" she whispered, although the brush of his hands around the tops of her boots sent sensual shivers all the way to her toes.

"Remember what I said about our first time together?" He slid the first zipper down in slow motion, teasing the inside of her thigh with his knuckle in the wake of the parting material. "No leather, no candles, no trappings. Just you and me."

"And the sound of our breathing." The words slipped from her mouth without thought.

He peered up as he tugged off her first boot. "You remember that speech?"

She remembered all right. His words to her that day in the Beachcomber's back room had haunted her dreams—waking *and* sleeping. She shrugged, knowing perfectly well he wouldn't believe her nonchalant guise. "I'll admit your claim to 'no tricks' intrigued me just a little."

"I've intrigued you." His fingers edged their way inside her other boot, then pulled the zipper slowly south to leave her barefoot on the polished hardwood floor of his bedroom. "Is that all I've managed to do, Noelle?"

A gorgeous man knelt at her feet, his shadowed jaw lurking inches from her bare thigh. It was all she could do not to melt.

"You've tempted me." Her voice cracked with the understatement.

He rose to stand, lifting her hair away from her ear and leaning close. "You've made my mouth water."

Noelle rocked back on her heels, no more boots to blame if she sank to the floor. She was two months away from turning forty and for the first time in her life, a man was making her swoon.

His arms went around her, steadying her, melding her body to his in slow degrees. She'd imagined the way he'd feel against her, and he was every bit of muscle she had dreamed and more. Fishing had her full approval if it gave men shoulders like these. She'd never felt so engulfed, protected…hot…in a man's embrace.

He tipped her head back to kiss her and she closed her eyes, waiting. She'd been bold enough for one night to show up at his doorstep and throw herself at him. She didn't mind letting him take the lead just now.

Not when his vision of their first night together had sounded so sweetly erotic.

He tasted her with a slow thoroughness that left her breathless. Her mind clouded to everything else but his kiss, so much so that she was surprised to find herself half out of her dress and falling gently backward into his bed a few moments later.

"I brought condoms just in case," she whispered, peering anxiously around the room for her leather jacket. "I stopped at the grocery store on my way here."

"You bought condoms at Twin Palms's only supermarket dressed like this?" She detected the amusement in his voice, even as he kissed his way down her neck to her bared breasts.

How could she think, much less string a sentence together when his tongue swept over her collarbone. "I went to a new guy—a cashier who didn't know who I was."

Brock slid her dress down her hips and let the

silver lace fall to the floor, leaving her clad only in her panties. His gaze moved over her with the thoroughness of a caress, lingering in all the places she longed for him most.

He didn't look any more capable of talking than she felt at the moment. His hands outlined her shoulders, skimmed her waist before he managed, "This is Twin Palms, Noelle. He'll know who you are by tomorrow."

"Do you care?"

"Are you kidding?" He pulled her to him all the tighter. "I'm hauling you to breakfast at the doughnut shop tomorrow morning to make sure everyone knows who was the lucky recipient of your cautious preparations."

He bent his head to her breast. His tongue swirled circles around her nipple, causing her back to arch right off the bed in greedy search for more. Trails of fire steamed through her to mingle with the unbearable heat between her legs.

She drew her fingers over his shoulder, tugged at his cotton T-shirt. "I'm not letting you out of bed until dinnertime at least, so that may present a problem."

He answered with a guttural groan that pleased her tremendously. He pulled off her panties and tossed aside all of his own clothes save a pair of black cotton boxers. She'd thought his muscles had *felt* spectacular, but looking at him proved even more delicious. She smoothed hungry fingers over him, eager to absorb every nuance of his magnificent body.

But no matter how much she teased and tormented

him with her fingers or her lips, Noelle discovered Brock could not be hurried. He teased and tormented right back, this man of delicious patience.

Only after he'd urged her to the edge of boat-rocking release twice did he retrieve the condoms from Noelle's coat pocket. She watched in rapt, hungry fascination as he ditched his boxers and sheathed himself for her. She met his gaze as he lay over her and pushed himself inside her.

No leather, no lingerie and no trappings proved every bit as sensual and seductive as she'd imagined. She'd never been so completely connected to any man, probably because they were pledging so much more than their bodies to one another.

The one trick Brock showed her she'd never seen before was his absolute, obvious love. A love she gave right back to him in every way she knew how.

True to his word, her gentle, patient lover made her cry out—not once, but time and time again that night—filling her with so much heat she could have sworn the walls had caught flame.

14

MIA LINED UP a new nail and pounded it into the simple wooden frame that would showcase her newest painting. She had been working feverishly all afternoon in the back of a rental van she'd used to haul her paintings to the Woodwin gallery in Ybor City, an artsy section of Tampa that catered to the young and hip.

Outside the van, she could hear the buzz of the Friday nightlife start to hum through the streets. Music drifted from two nearby bars, Caribbean drums from the left mixing with jazz riffs from the right to create a uniquely Floridian sound.

Instead of inspiring her creativity however, the music only agitated her nerves all the more. She had one chance to make tonight a success, to impress art buyers and to realize a profit on the work she'd been producing over the past three years. She wished tonight had been a little more about artistic satisfaction and less about a bottom line, but at least she still had an opportunity to save the Beachcomber before the store spiraled into foreclosure and broke her grandparents' hearts.

She only hoped Seth would arrive soon before her

own heart broke tonight. How had he become so important to her in such a short amount of time?

Eyeing the canvas in the frame she'd hastily put together, Mia wondered where he could be and why he'd chosen to leave Twin Palms the week before her art show. Granted, she hadn't talked much about the show or really stressed how important tonight would be for her. But she'd invited him when he called her two nights ago to say his business in Tampa would be delayed a little longer.

Before she could ruminate over Seth or the semi-crooked picture any longer, a sudden banging on the outside of the van made her jump.

"How's the artist holding up in there?" Noelle shouted from among the jumbled mix of voices on the street. Thankfully, Noelle hadn't held a grudge after Mia lost her temper earlier in the week. Her mother hadn't even indulged in their usual mutual sulking after an argument.

She'd been too flat-out thrilled with her new relationship with Brock Chandler and her commitment to a moped rental shop in Twin Palms. Mia still couldn't believe her rebel mom was ready to put down a root or two. She couldn't help feeling a twinge of jealousy for what Noelle had found with Brock. She was fast realizing she wanted that sort of love for herself. Forever.

Mia gently set aside her painting to pry open the backdoor of the van. The sound of music and noise from traffic on the interstate nearby echoed through the vehicle.

Outside, her mother stood hand in hand with

Brock while she balanced a huge bouquet of snap-dragons and lilies.

"Congratulations and good luck!" she shouted with a double dose of Noelle-exuberance.

"They're gorgeous!" Mia reached for the vase, touched by her mother's gesture. At the same time, her conscience pricked at the fact that she hadn't apologized to Noelle yet for the blowout at the beach. Not that Noelle looked like she was thinking about that moment just now. Mia's mother had never looked so outrageously happy, and even Brock's gruff fisherman scowl softened to something close to a smile whenever he was near Noelle. Anyone could see they were head over heels for one another.

Mia couldn't help but think they looked like she and Seth might look if Seth ever wanted more than a live-in girlfriend. Assuming, that is, if she ever saw him again.

"Hi, Mom." Before Mia could think about her show, or Seth, however, she needed to do some serious apologizing. She settled the flower arrangement on an empty crate in the back of the van. "Can you spare a couple of minutes to, you know, talk?"

Brock held up his hand and backed away, slowly. "Sounds like girl stuff to me. I'll go check out that bongo player and catch up with you in five." He planted a kiss on Noelle's cheek. "Good luck tonight, Mia."

Noelle uttered a dreamy sigh as he walked away. "I'm totally in love," she admitted, hitching at the strap of her funky orange cocktail dress with a skinny rhinestone belt. "Big time."

Any jealousy Mia might have felt took a definite back seat to her genuine joy for what her mother had found. Noelle deserved some happiness after such a rocky start.

In fact, as Mia looked at her mom, so caught up in new love, she seemed to see her with new eyes. They really weren't that far apart in age. She'd always known that intellectually, but seeing her mother looking so energized and happy made Mia realize how truly young Noelle had been when she'd had her only child.

"I'm happy for you. He's a great guy." Mia offered her hand. "Come on in and sit for a minute."

Noelle grimaced, her mouth turning into an exaggerated frown. "You're not going to put me to work making frames or stretching canvas or anything that's messy or—?"

Mia took a deep breath for courage. "I'm going to apologize for being incredibly clueless and not figuring out earlier in life that you only left me with Grammie and Grandpa because you felt like you didn't have a choice."

Noelle's jaw fell wide open. It took her a minute to recover.

"Okay." Noelle took Mia's hand. "That's definitely a conversation we ought to have. Messy or not." She pulled herself into the van and plunked down onto the brown vinyl bench seat against one wall. "But you're not the one who needs to apologize."

"Oh that's right. It was you who threw the big

tantrum on the beach.'' Mia rolled her eyes. ''Come on, Mom. How often do I admit I'm wrong?''

Noelle smiled. ''Hardly ever. Which only makes sense considering you come from a proud line of stubborn Quentins, missy, and don't you forget it.'' She poked Mia's kneecap with the toe of her rhinestone-covered shoe. ''But as long as we're settling up old wrongs,'' she reached over to give Mia's hand a quick squeeze. ''I think it's far past time for me to say how sorry I am for making such crappy choices when you were a baby.''

Mia blinked. Twice. ''Mom, you don't have to—''

''Yes I do.'' She clutched her purse in a white-knuckled grip, her gaze steady and serious. ''And this is tough enough for me as it is, so let me just blurt it on out here.''

Mia waited, silent. Gave her mom an encouraging nod.

''I should have talked to you a long time ago, but I kept thinking you weren't old enough to really understand why I did what I did.'' Noelle picked at the rhinestones on her clutch purse, no doubt plagued with as much fear of eye contact as Mia was feeling right about now. ''Of course, I should have known I was just making excuses since you were *born* more mature than me.''

No witty replies came to mind. No teasing jibes to sling back at her mother to keep everything light and superficial. And even if she could have thought of some neat response, Mia would have had a difficult time voicing it over the lump in her throat.

Noelle looked up and met Mia's gaze head on.

"Leaving you was the hardest thing I've ever done in my life. And I guess it's only just started to hit home for me this week that you've really never known that."

Tears itched the back of Mia's eyes. Big, hot tears she didn't have a chance of hiding. She slid onto the brown vinyl seat beside her mother and stared straight ahead at a crooked, half finished canvas she'd stuffed in the van. "It couldn't have been easy for you, having a baby at sixteen."

Noelle shook her head. "*Having* the baby was cake compared to walking away from my little girl. I will always regret letting your grandmother steam-roll me on that one, Mia, but please know that I only did it because I thought they could do a better job taking care of you than I would have. I couldn't have supported you alone, but I shouldn't have let them push me right out of your life. I should have been there for you, too."

The tears spilled over in gushing streams from Mia's eyes, rounding her cheeks and curling under her jaw. She reached for her mother's hand. Finding it, she held on tightly, reconnecting them as mother and daughter.

They cried for a few moments, silent and side by side. Mia laid her head on her Noelle's shoulder, not even caring that the rhinestones would leave little tracks right across her temple.

Finally, Noelle handed her a tissue. "You'd better start getting ready, hon. I don't want to screw up your big night."

Mia nodded, swiping away the mascara she knew

must be smudged under her eyes. "Grammie and Grandpa were proud of you, you know. Even when you were throwing all sorts of rebel motorcycle boyfriends in their faces."

Mia retreated to talking about her grandparents, knowing she couldn't confide how much she'd missed her mother in her early years. Besides, she had the feeling those years apart had cost Noelle far more than they'd cost Mia.

"Really?" Noelle sniffled, wiping tears off her own cheeks.

"Grandpa gave out Beachcomber matchbooks to everyone who came in the store the day he found out you made the Dean's list at Indiana University."

"Get out." Noelle elbowed her in the arm. "Are we talking about the same Norman Quentin?"

Mia laughed, rising to her feet. "Yup. But I'm saving all my other secrets for a day when I don't have to make a big impression on the Tampa artistic community. I'm never going to hide the puffy eyes, as it is, thank you very much." She reached for the frame she'd been trying to put together before her mother arrived, grateful for something to fidget with to burn off her nervousness.

Noelle nodded, a wordless acceptance of the new peace between them. "Good idea. How can I help?"

"Is Seth here?" The question popped out of Mia's mouth before she could think about how pathetic she sounded.

"Not yet. But everybody else in town is inside. Cocktail hour only just kicked in but there's already a good crowd." Noelle eyed her daughter up and down. "No offense, Madam Artist, but is that what you're wearing to your first gallery showing?"

Mia stared down at her jean shorts and T-shirt. "Guess I got caught up in the details. Could you do anything to help this painting while I dig around for my dress?"

Noelle took the frame from Mia. "I'll get Brock to help me put this together."

"Cool. Love ya, mom." Mia kissed Noelle's cheek.

"Right back at ya, Mia." Noelle winked. "Now go!"

Mia unearthed her dress and makeup bag and sidled around Noelle to jump down from the van and access the gallery through the alley entrance.

As she searched for the private lounge in the back of the building, Mia tried not to think how much less stressed she'd be tonight if Seth had been here. She would have liked his business-savvy presence to guide her through tonight's daunting crowd. Even if he'd just assure her that her paintings didn't suck, that her work would appeal to someone in Tampa, or that she wouldn't be a total failure in life if she didn't make enough money tonight to save the Beachcomber, she would have been most grateful.

Finding the small lounge, Mia shoved the door open and nearly fell right into her pirate-turned-corporate shark.

Seth stood in the shadows of her dressing room, crisp and gorgeous in a charcoal suit that probably cost as much as her entire wardrobe. His tie was a silkscreen copy of Monet's *Waterlilies,* however, a nice nod to tonight's occasion.

"Sorry I'm late."

He barely got the words out when she tackled him. She flung herself into his arms and knocked him back at least three feet. He smelled like aftershave and soap and everything about him felt rock solid against her.

"I missed you." She stretched up on her toes to kiss him but he was already leaning over her, cupping the back of her neck with one hand and tugging her closer by the waist with the other.

His mouth moved over hers with a hunger, a need to possess, as greedy as her own.

He pulled away from her too soon, leaving her dizzy with want and more than a little muddled. She became vaguely aware of their surroundings, the small rolltop desk in one corner of the private lounge and an overstuffed sofa in the other. The door to the bathroom she'd been seeking was situated between two bright blue Picasso reproductions.

"If I don't stop now, I won't be able to stop." His words whispered through her passion-fogged brain cells.

"I don't know how I'm going to get through the show." Her senses tingled, vibrantly alert to Seth's touch, his scent, his taste.

"It's worse for men, Mia. Trust me." He looked so serious she couldn't help but laugh.

"That's an old line, Seth. I'm not a sixteen-year-old on a parking date, you know. I think you'll manage." She shook out the dress she was holding and eyed the new wrinkles critically. She had forgotten all about it when she'd flung herself into Seth's arms. "Besides, you're the one who left *me* for days on end. A little suffering serves you right."

Mia pushed the bathroom door open so she could change into her dress and comb out her hair while catching up with Seth.

"I've got a good surprise for you to show for it, though." He peered through the open bathroom door just as she pulled off her T-shirt. "Need any help in here?"

She threw her T-shirt at him. "Not if I want to make an appearance at this thing. They're probably already wondering where I am." She slid into her black tailored cocktail dress and then pulled her shorts off from under the skirt. "Now what's this about a surprise for me?

Seth whistled appreciatively at her transformation. "Just a little something to take the pressure off you tonight." He reached into his pocket and withdrew a long envelope tied with a red ribbon. "Do you have time to open it before you go out there?"

Curious, she finished combing her hair and whipped on a coat of muted red lipstick. "I always have time for a surprise."

She plucked the envelope out of his hand, and tested the weight. It was heavier, thicker than she'd expected. "I'm hoping this is a promise of explicit sexual favors redeemable in about three hours from now."

"Unfortunately, I wasn't nearly that creative. But

you have my word the sexual favors are a given."
His gaze roamed over her, restless and edgy.

She smiled back at him as she slid off the ribbon
and tucked her finger inside the envelope to pull out
the sheaf of papers.

Important, legal-looking papers.

Mia squinted down at the tiny printing on the front
page of a stapled document that looked to be signed
and notarized on the bottom. What on earth?

"Property at 6 Ocean Drive, Twin Palms Florida—" she read aloud until the moment her brain
fully processed what she held in her hands. Her stomach churned as her blood cooled a few frosty degrees.

"This is the deed to the Beachcomber."

Perhaps her horror showed in her face, because
Seth's engaging grin flipped to a frown. "I shuffled
around the Gulf Coast account so that you wouldn't
have to worry about foreclosure."

When she didn't—couldn't—say anything in response to that, he shrugged. "Technically, you now
have a loan directly from Chandler Enterprises instead—a company I can guarantee will give you
some latitude to get the Beachcomber back in the
black."

Hurt seeped through her in a slow, aching tide.

"You mean technically you now own my store."
And no matter how Mia viewed it, Seth's announce-
ment came as the final sign that he didn't have any
interest in a real partnership with her. Did she need
to realize that on this night that already felt too sig-
nificant, too make-or-break her career to bear? Hurt
made her lash out, careless of her words. "And tech-

nically, by sleeping with you, I'm pretty much whoring my way out of foreclosure, right?''

"Hell, no, Mia." His gaping jaw in the wake of her reaction assured her he hadn't thought about their deal in those terms. "I just thought it would be pretty simple for me to take the pressure off you so you didn't get too stressed about the fate of the store. It's not a big deal to shuffle accounts around in my business."

"It's my account." She heard the waver in her voice, a direct result of her effort not to weep with frustration that he'd never be the kind of man to share any kind of control with her. Was it so much to ask for a little faith in her ability to know what she was doing? "And you had no right to touch it."

Despite the generosity of his gesture, and with more than a little regret, she shoved the papers, ribbon and all, back into his hands and walked out of the bathroom.

"It's not like I broke any bank policies." He followed her out into the small office lounge, stuffing the Beachcomber deed back into his jacket and oblivious to what his actions implied for her. "Once an account is behind in payments, the bank always has the option to sell off the note to another creditor. I just thought I might be an easier business for you to deal with now."

Mia stopped at the door. She needed to meet the public and start promoting her work at this show, but she couldn't just walk away from Seth like this either. She'd let her temper get the better of her with her mother this week and regretted it later.

She took calming breaths and tried to put her situation in terms Seth would understand.

"I understand that you meant to help, but I'm frustrated that you didn't have enough faith in me to take care of my own business." Major understatement. But what purpose would it serve to tell him his white knight act had made her feel all-but-damn-helpless on a night that might have been a triumph for her? "Also, I think it is glaringly apparent that since we are now doing business together, we won't be sleeping together anymore."

She couldn't share herself with a man interested in calling all the shots—a man for whom "partnership" was a foreign notion.

"Mia wait."

He reached for her, but she pulled open the door to step into the gallery humming with activity and cocktail conversation.

She shot him a level gaze, unwilling to be placated with his overdeveloped protective instincts or—God forbid—the gorgeous brown eyes she'd been seeing in her dreams all week. "I'll be sure to drop my first payment in the mail to you on Monday."

A LONG, LOW WHISTLE emanated from behind Seth as he lingered half in the gallery hallway and half in the doorway to the lounge, watching Mia walk away from him with long, angry strides.

He turned to find Brock and Noelle standing in the alleyway entrance, both a bit wide-eyed. Brock held one of Mia's smaller paintings in his hand.

"I take it you heard that?"

Brock nodded. "Just something about mailing you money, which made no sense. But she could have been spouting Romanian and we still would have figured out she's mad enough to chew nails—or unsuspecting Chandlers at the very least."

Noelle eased the painting out of Brock's hand. "I'd better go see where she wants to hang this." Shooting a sympathetic look in Seth's direction, Noelle followed Mia toward the gallery.

"I moved the Beachcomber's loan so that it's a private holding for Chandler Enterprises," Seth admitted once Noelle was out of hearing distance. Not that she wouldn't learn the facts of this argument soon enough. "She's furious."

Brock shook his head. "A loan like that might be just another entry in the company checkbook for you, kid, but for her it's huge. How would you have felt when you were starting out ten years ago if you were working your butt off for that first million and somebody just came in and handed it to you instead? Would you feel the same way about achieving your objective?"

"That's a dumb-ass comparison."

"It's a freaking brilliant comparison." Brock thunked Seth on the shoulder. "You just robbed her of her chance to make this all turn out right on her own."

"Is it so wrong to want to take the pressure off? Shit, Brock, if she doesn't come through with this money, her business is a prime target for corporate raiding. Some hungry investor could see that prop-

erty hanging on the verge of foreclosure next week
and snap it up like that.''

He snapped his fingers, the strength of his own
convictions returning the more he thought about what
he'd done. ''Don't you think it would be worse to
be robbed of the chance to turn the business around
altogether? You know how sought after beachfront
property is. Somebody could bulldoze the whole
damn building and put up some obnoxious hotel in
the middle of Twin Palms. Would that be better?''

He stalked toward the alley exit, needing to get
the hell out of the gallery. No doubt, Mia wouldn't
want him there now.

''You could have explained that to her before you
took the decision out of her hands,'' Brock called
after him. ''Better yet, you could have just *asked* her
if she wanted your help.''

The words echoed in Seth's ears, not that he paid
any attention to them.

The steam all but rose from Seth's head as he
stepped out into the busy Ybor City street. Mia was
mad. Brock was mad. Hell, didn't he have any right
to be mad about this too? He'd been in business for
ten years moving money around every day of his
damn life. Couldn't he get any credit that he knew
exactly what he was doing when it came to corporate
finance?

He rounded the corner of the alley and headed
toward the front of the gallery's brick facade. His
steps slowed as he reached a street-level window
looking into tonight's showing.

The pale walls of the main gallery highlighted

Mia's paintings to their best advantage. The vivid colors that were a mainstay of her work leaped off the canvas to fill the room with a sense of motion and vibrancy.

Her fairy-tale composition hung in between a romantic interpretation of Cupid and Psyche and a cartoonish rendering of the University of Tampa. In her version of the campus, there were no students roaming the courtyard, but Moorish nineteenth century figures to match the building's dramatic architecture.

It was clever and different and uniquely Mia. Her vision of the world was sensual and artistic while his had always been, admittedly, bottom-line practical. She wanted to take a few calculated risks in life now, while he was working diligently to make sure she didn't get hurt.

Maybe his approach hadn't been the greatest, but at least his motives were laudable.

Still, he'd been consigned—literally—to the status of an outsider looking in. But for the first time in any of his relationships with women, he wouldn't accept his walking papers. Mia had ended things with him in no uncertain terms tonight, but this time, he wouldn't be satisfied to write her off as a failed relationship and move on.

Mia Quentin was a woman worth fighting for. A woman for keeps.

And holy hell, Seth loved her.

The assurance of that emotion squeezed his chest like a vise and convinced him he'd better find a way to make things right with her, and for her, again.

Which meant he couldn't stand around gawking at her through windows like some Armani-clad peeping Tom.

He had work to do.

15

MIA SMOOTHED restless fingers over her new white eyelet dress and stood in the middle of the Beachcomber's new pine hardwood floor to survey her last three days of frenzied work.

On the day of the gift shop's grand reopening, high-end bath products and all-natural sea salts shared shelf space with organic sponges in every shape and size. Thick terry cloth beach towels in a rainbow of colors took the place of the "My Grandma Went to Florida and All I Got Was This Lousy Towel" inventory. Best of all, Mia's few paintings left over from her gallery show now lined the lavender walls, not a single pink flamingo in sight.

A simple pine treasure chest held Gasparilla memorabilia in one corner of the store, the lone domain she'd given to her grandfather to stock however he pleased.

Thinking of Gasparilla and her encounter with a certain sexy pirate only depressed her, however.

"Don't think about him," Noelle prompted from her spot behind the counter. She studied the cash register's computer screen like an eighth-grader poised over her first biology dissection before sending Mia a grin. "You ought to be celebrating your successes today instead of thinking about the one that got away."

"I agree," Mia's grandmother shouted from the back room. She swept into store carrying an armful of inflatable toys, her face half-buried behind alligators and Shamu knockoffs. "Sweetheart, are you sure we don't have a place for these? They are always such good sellers."

Mia took the toys out of her grandmother's arms and staggered behind the front counter with the heavy pile. "How about we keep them back here and you can give them away to any families with children today?" Not giving Betty time to argue, Mia turned her attention back to Noelle. "And whatever gave you the idea Seth is the one who got away? He's the one I helped on his way, Mother, because he was too controlling and too—"

"Too helpful?" Betty offered.

"Too gorgeous?" Noelle supplied, enjoying this far too much.

"Too smothering," Mia corrected them, earning a loud snort from her grandfather on his folding chair behind the counter where he played a round of solitaire.

"Oh honestly, Mia," Betty chided, stacking the wayward alligators more neatly next to the register. "You feel smothered because a nice man goes out of his way to do you a favor?"

"No, I—"

"Or do you feel scared to be in a relationship with a nice man you really care about because he might not be able to commit to you?'' Noelle folded her arms and scrutinized her daughter.

Now Mia felt like the object of the eighth-grader's dissection. And part of her couldn't help but fear her mother might be right.

"Hardly. Mother, you haven't scarred me for life half as much you think you have." She did *not* have abandonment issues, thank you very much. Ever since she and Noelle had come to a new understanding, Mia felt a little more relaxed about her past. Maybe a little more open to her future.

She just wished it didn't have to be without Seth.

Her eyes swept the store, searching for the slightest thing out of place before she flipped the sign on the front door to "Open." There was nothing. "I just can't be with someone who wants to protect me from all of life. The three of you already have that covered."

Norman paused in the midst of his solitaire game. "But none of us know a blasted thing about foreclosure laws or banking, Mia. We wouldn't have had a clue how to protect the store from corporate raiders or money-hungry investors if someone had gotten wind of this place being in trouble. You could give the damn pirate some credit for at least knowing his business."

Norman hadn't voiced an opinion beyond a grunt in years. While Mia and Noelle scraped their jaws off the floor, Betty shrugged.

"Must be all those fishing outings are making him a bit salty," she suggested, patting his shoulder absently.

"Damn refreshing to talk to someone besides a shop full of women," Norman grumbled, returning to his cards as is he hadn't just flipped Mia's perception of Seth on its ear.

Had she been too hasty to jump all over Seth for interfering? Heck, no. The Beachcomber was *her* business. Well, at least until it got back on its feet and she could pass it back to her grandparents.

She looked around the renovated gift shop and wondered if that task would be more difficult than she'd anticipated. Her hard work the past two weeks had made her realize how much she enjoyed the place. It had always been filled with love—even when she'd resented the workload as a child, she'd appreciated that her grandparents wanted to share their dream with her.

She hadn't forgotten those dreams. She had plans to clear out the back room and use it as a children's shop with all the fun, touristy stuff her grandparents had always stocked their shelves with. In a few more weeks, Norman could sit in his folding chair back there and show the kids how to work the wind-up manatees and remote-control toy jet skis.

Now, the new look of the store gave her more than a sense of family. It had transformed into a place of beauty and a delight to the senses. Her paintings warmed the walls with color and movement. Even the coat of lavender beneath them showcased the work in a more exciting light than the flat white walls of the downtown art gallery.

The scent of the sea wafted in the windows, mingling with lemon-scented wood polish and fragrant bath salts. And all she had to do was trail a fingertip over the bins of sponges and loofahs, scratchy pumice stones and velvety beach towels for another enticing sensory experience.

The Beachcomber was now a sensualist's ideal playground and the perfect home for her art. And for some stupid reason, she'd thought she'd be able to walk away from it.

Just like she'd walked away from Seth. Had that been a really ill-advised move, too?

No, damn it. He should have consulted her before moving around her banknote. In the long run, she'd probably saved them both some heartache anyway. She had already been starting to fall for Seth. If they'd gotten any closer, she would have ended up another casualty on his string of women he protected and felt responsible for, but never cared about enough to offer a true partnership.

Absently, Mia looked out the front door and was surprised to see a small throng of beach goers congregated outside on the porch. She thrust thoughts of Seth aside—although memories of him were never any further than that damn treasure chest loaded with daggers and eye patches—and focused on welcoming customers.

A steady stream of traffic kept her store full and her cash register moving. By noon, Noelle was operating the computer like a pro, making change and doling out beauty advice to anyone who purchased skin care items.

Norman had put his air compressor to work nonstop on the front porch, inflating the giveaway ride-on toys to the children in the crowd. Betty had whispered to Mia more than once that she should have been charging for the toys, but Mia couldn't help but think she would be getting her money back in good P.R. value.

Where all the customers came from, Mia hadn't a clue. They'd never done this much business in her lifetime. They'd barely ever done this much business on a good week before, let alone in a day. She vaguely credited the journalists who'd attended her gallery showing for putting something in their newspapers about the grand reopening of the store along with their stories about her art.

But while Mia was straightening up the pawed-through sponge display, she overheard a couple of bikini-clad beach bunnies discussing a megahot pirate on the beach and began to wonder if she owed her stream of customers to a very different source.

After all, how many megahot pirates could there be on the South Florida coast these days?

Surely she'd misheard. She had pirates on the brain thanks to that damn treasure chest—a display case she vowed to hide in the back room tonight to eliminate some of her Seth daydreams.

As if that would help.

Smiling, Mia approached the two girls—a redhead in purple flowers and a brunette wearing navy and white stripes—who couldn't have been more than nineteen or twenty years old.

"Excuse me." Mia's heart pounded—with hope

or massive trepidation, she couldn't be sure. "Did I hear you mention something about a pirate?"

Was it Mia's imagination, or did the whole store just turn quiet? She whipped around to look at her mother at the cash register, who stared back at her for a split second before pushing a flurry of buttons to set the machine beeping back at her.

Suspicion knotted her stomach.

Nodding, the redhead grinned. "That pirate you hired to promote the store out on the beach is totally gorgeous." She elbowed her friend and continued digging through the sponge display. "He can jolly his Roger with me any time."

The girls giggled, oblivious to Mia's rising tide of fury.

"What is he doing to promote the store exactly?" He would interfere in her business again, after she'd specifically told him not to? After she'd walked away from him, much to the detriment of her own heart?

There would be hell to pay if Seth Chandler was outside her store today.

The brunette stood up straighter. "He's not doing anything he shouldn't be. He's just sort of passing out flyers about the store and the legend of Pirate Don Jose."

Mia's icy anger thawed just a little. "Don Jose?"

"Not exactly as intimidating as Blackbeard, is it?" the redhead agreed.

No, not exactly. But then, the opera character of Carmen had never wanted Blackbeard. She'd been in love with a certain Spanish captain named Don Jose.

"But the legend of the pirate is so romantic," the

brunette fanned herself, sighing dreamily. "I'd take Don Jose in a heartbeat."

"Do you happen to have a copy of this legend?" Mia asked, curious. Not that any romantic wooing from Seth was going to convince her she should hand over the reins of her business to a man who never bothered to consult her.

But it couldn't hurt to at least read what he'd written before she sent him and his eye patch packing.

SETH CIRCLED his boat around the cove he'd discovered just up the coast from Twin Palms and headed back to the marina to drop off his latest passengers. People were really buying into the legend of Pirate Don Jose, so much so that beachgoers of all ages had begged him to show them the supposed site where Don Jose and Carmen had pledged their love to one another.

Everyone that is, except for Mia, who hadn't so much as stepped out of the store all day.

So after raining tons of flyers around Twin Palms to promote the reopening of Mia's store, Seth had dutifully loaded up interested romantics for a boat trip past the cove he'd discovered yesterday. Every woman he'd paraded out there had gazed longingly at the site.

Damn it, where was the only woman that mattered?

Seth scanned the shoreline as he neared Twin Palms Beach. No sign of Mia.

Frustrated, he turned his attention toward the marina to drop off his passengers. And then he saw a lone woman on the dock. A lone woman in a filmy white dress with a red hibiscus tucked behind one ear.

Mia.

Seth steered the cabin cruiser into the marina as fast as he dared, gliding up to the narrow finger dock behind Brock's fishing vessel. He hitched a rope to the cleat and tossed the fenders overboard to keep the boat from scraping the dock, then stepped onto the planked pier behind his last departing passenger—an older woman of about sixty who winked back at Seth.

"There's a Carmen if ever I've seen one," she stage-whispered. "I hope you're going to show *her* the cove."

Seth nodded, but his thoughts were too focused on Mia to string together any kind of coherent response.

Her white dress revealed lots of tanned, golden skin and provided a stark contrast to her dark brown hair. Thin silver bracelets jingled on one wrist, while a silver chain decorated with little charms circled her ankle. In her hand, she clutched a copy of the flyer he'd been passing out—the one with the Beachcomber promotional stuff on one side, and the legend of Don Jose on the other.

She waved the piece of paper at him. "I see you're back to making business decisions without me."

She might look delicate as a hothouse flower in her pristine white dress, but she had the spitfire instincts of her opera heroine namesake.

"I'd like to think my marketing efforts were a big help to business today." Damn it, if she wasn't pulling punches, neither would he. "That front door of yours looked awfully active from my spot on the beach."

"We had an incredible day." She lifted her chin into the wind, allowing the warm breeze to curl through her hair and fan her filmy skirt. "But I still don't think it's right for you to take business initiatives without consulting me."

"I agree."

He could tell his head-on damage control surprised her. She turned to face him, disrupting the way the breeze blew across her and inadvertently inviting a few feet of hair to wrap around her neck like a scarf while other strands blew over her eyes.

Patiently, she lifted the stray pieces out of her vision and studied him with interest.

"I see now I messed up by switching the accounts around without asking you. I'm used to shuffling stuff like that every day in my business, so it didn't seem like a big deal at the time. In hindsight, I realize I had no right to touch any of your business dealings without asking."

Her eyes widened. She held up the flyer in her hands. "Then why did you march right in today and pull the same stunt again by advertising on my behalf without ever consulting me?"

"I needed to show you I have good business sense, Mia, and I was afraid if I asked you this time you'd shoot me down without ever letting me prove it to you."

He could tell his reasoning didn't come close to swaying her. The frown on her face conveyed volumes.

"So you commit the same mistake twice to prove a point?"

"Hell no, Mia. I might have sent people to your shop today, but your work still had to stand on its own." He'd left the final control in her hands. Her talented, artistic hands.

She said nothing, but he could tell by her clear-eyed gaze that she was thinking, weighing, considering. He forged on, knowing this would be a now-or-never chance to tell her his side.

He had the feeling he wouldn't win this round on determination alone. If he wanted to sway Mia, he'd have to lay it all on the line and let her decide.

"Look, I realize I had no right to touch your accounts, but I felt pretty certain you'd be forgiving about me directing a slew of new business to the store today, even if I hadn't asked first."

He wanted to touch her, to skim his fingers over her lips, her smooth, bared shoulder, the flower in her hair. But he knew it was too soon. He clenched his hands into fists and forged through his explanation, hoping he didn't sound like the world's most conceited guy. "And damn it, Mia, I just wanted a chance to show you I know a thing or two about business. I messed up by not talking to you about it first, but my gut told me not to leave that debt sitting there for any stray corporate raider to scoop up in a foreclosure. Real estate like this goes in a blink, and then you'd be out of luck for a lifetime. I was so focused on fixing that, I didn't stop to weigh the consequences."

She studied him like a stubborn stretch of canvas

that wouldn't quite conform to her color scheme. He just hoped she didn't paint him and his troublesome self right out of the damn picture.

"It's a mistake I would never make again," he offered. "If given the chance, of course."

Mia shook her head, her expression inscrutable. She turned her chin back into the wind and looked out over the ocean.

"I don't like it, but I guess I can understand it." Her words were soft, diffused by the sea breeze.

Before he could decide whether or not that meant she'd forgiven him, she fixed him with a direct stare, her green eyes unwavering.

"You're giving tours now?" Mia raised an eyebrow, but her expression lacked the anger of the other night. She crossed her arms over her chest, as if waiting to be impressed.

He'd wanted one more chance, and clearly, she was going to give him an opportunity. Now, with his future riding on his ability to make things right, the pressure not to screw up was twenty times more intense than any last-minute shot at the buzzer he'd ever taken.

This time it counted a hell of a lot more.

MIA WAITED, knowing she couldn't act on impulse anymore with Seth. She wanted to jump him now as much as she ever had, especially with that familiar eye patch shoved up above his brow, unused. And God knew, the smooth, toned muscles of his once-again bared chest or the bristly dark hair on his thighs weren't exactly helping her to stay strong.

But she wasn't just looking for one wild night anymore. She feared she wanted a whole lot more than Seth was prepared to give her, but it didn't hurt to at least talk to him one last time.

Seth checked his watch. "You're in luck. I give private tours only after five o'clock. You game?"

Mia looked back at the Beachcomber. Her family would need to close the store on their own at six if she left. Three weeks ago she would have been scared they'd kill one another in her absence. Now there was a distinct possibility they'd all share a stack of gyros on Brock's boat and hash out plans for Noelle's new business.

All of a sudden, Mia felt like the only emotional misfit in the family.

"I'm game." She held out her hand to Seth, allowing him to help her on board. Their first time on a boat together, she'd had to practically drag him into coming along with her. Now she was the one with reservations. "I figure I owe it to myself to see where Carmen and Don Jose got together since I've got a bit of an affinity with the Carmen half of the duo."

"You two could be sisters," Seth agreed, firing up the boat while Mia settled herself on a cushion near the rail.

"You seem very familiar with these characters." Mia lifted her chin into the warm Gulf breeze as they motored slowly out of the marina and headed up the coast.

The salt water sprayed her cheeks and shoulders, while the wind dried it on her skin seconds later. The sun sat low in the sky, casting a path of yellow light on turquoise water.

He shrugged. "They're based on real people I know pretty well."

Mia lifted the flyer she'd read through three times already. "It says here Don Jose kidnapped Carmen and then she fell in love with him while he was her captor."

He turned to her, his serious expression betraying no hint of teasing. "Prisoner's syndrome. I hear that really happens sometimes."

Mia's heart lightened as they sped along the water. This was what had attracted to her Seth from day one. The man had a latent adventurous spirit just waiting for her to nudge it into action.

"Actually, I've heard the reverse is true." She removed her soggy hibiscus from her hair and shook off the excess water from the damp petals. "It's quite easy for an abductor to fall in love with his captive. He starts out thinking he's got all the power in a relationship, but then his feelings begin to work against him and it turns out the captive is the one wielding all the power."

Seth slowed the boat and turned it into a cove she'd never noticed before, but she guessed it couldn't be more than a few miles from the store. He edged the boat into the small inlet and dropped anchor about twenty-five feet from shore.

Only then did he turn to look at her, his dark brown gaze like a heated caress. "I can imagine that happening in a minute. But I suppose the best way to handle things would be to share the power."

"A little give and take is always a good thing." The words promptly stuck in her throat because her idea of give and take took an erotic turn in her mind, and inspired a highly arousing thought.

Which she would definitely squelch because they hadn't resolved much of anything yet.

Seth stood. "You look a little flushed, Mia. I think we could both use a nice cold dip on our way to the shore." He tugged her to her feet.

"You're kidding." The water was a dangerous place for them. The last time they'd tangled in the Gulf they'd ended up rolling around under the boardwalk like frenzied teenagers and Mia had all she could do to keep from falling in love with him.

No matter how cold the water was, she didn't think she'd survive round two.

But he was already taking off his shoes.

"Never let it be said I was the one who stifled the adventurous side of the corporate shark." She unbuttoned the top button of her dress.

He stared at her chest, transfixed for one heady moment. Then he scrambled to button the buttons back up.

"If we want to keep the balance of power even here, you're keeping this dress on." His jaw flexed in his intense concentration on those little pearl buttons.

Heat sparked through her at his touch.

"That's okay," she agreed standing politely still. Then she lowered her voice to the deliberately throaty range. "It will be just as effective when it's sopping wet in a few minutes."

His gaze looked so bleak one would think she'd just twisted a knife in the poor guy's back.

Ah, revenge.

"We are *talking*," he ground out through clenched teeth, pulling her toward the boat railing. "Now jump."

Before she had a chance to get her bearings, Seth scooped her off the deck and jumped with her. The water closed over her head for only a minute before Seth propelled them above the surface.

She sputtered, wiping her hair out of her eyes, her skin tingling with the cool temperature of the water. "Never jump into strange water," she admonished, her breathing coming in little gasps. "I may be adventurous, but I'm not crazy."

He flashed her a wicked grin and swam a few feet away. "I swam all over here yesterday when I discovered this place, Mia. I may be a bit of a planner, but I'm not crazy either. Come on."

She swam after him, her dress floating around and between her legs as she kicked her way through the water. The cove was covered with trees, the water protected by live oaks and a big banyan tree. The beach wasn't groomed, but it was still sandy and smoothed. A big rock loomed on one end, just flat enough to make an enticing spot to sit.

Mia pulled herself out of the water and lay back on it to catch her breath, closing her eyes for just a moment.

"You were right," Seth's voice drifted from above. "That dress is deadly when it's wet."

A smile grew inside her long before it reached her

lips. She propped an eyelid open to stare up at him, his gaze nowhere near her eyes. "Still want to talk?"

Any chill left over from the water dissipated under his sultry stare.

"Actually I've got about five other ideas in mind that sound damn appealing right now, but I'm hellbent on the talking." His voice hit a husky note that brought her nipples to attention and sizzled along her flesh.

She sat up, more than ready to listen to what he had would say. If it was more important than the electric flash sparking between them right now, it must be worth hearing.

He climbed onto the flat rock to sit beside her. "I signed your banknote over to Brock so you don't owe me anything. I know you hated the idea of me holding the note, so it's gone. You guys can work out a way for you to pay it off over the next few years at the going interest rate, if that sounds fair to you."

It sounded more than fair. It also sounded like the act of a guy who might be interested in preserving a relationship with her. But had he done it just so they could get back to the kind of relationship they had before? She wasn't so sure it would be enough anymore.

"You did that for me?"

"Not just me—Brock wanted to do it for you, too. I was going to sell the note to Jesse, but Brock said he's sticking around Twin Palms anyway, so it'll be easier for you to pay him."

"Does your whole family have money coming out

their ears that any one of them can afford to pick up this considerable debt of mine?''

Seth shrugged. ''I'm their investor, so they've done well along with me.''

Hard for her to comprehend, coming from a family who'd been in business a lifetime and still struggled to make ends meet. But Seth was really, wildly successful at what he did. ''My check from the art gallery went out today, so I should be able to pay off at least half of what I owe Brock by Friday.''

''You're kidding.'' Seth let loose a low whistle. ''You made that much on your first show?''

Pleasure warmed her to her toes. She'd been pretty happy with the outcome as well. ''The gallery wants to do another one in the spring.''

''Congratulations, Mia. You worked hard for this.'' Genuine admiration threaded through his words. He looked out at the sun starting to dip into the water.

The sky had transformed to indigo as they'd talked, and now a light pink tinged the horizon. A warm breeze continued to dry her dress, however, gently fanning the skirt as it blew in off the water.

She *had* worked hard for it. And now, as they watched the sunset in silence, it occurred to her that she'd produced more work in the weeks she'd known Seth than she had in the past three years. She'd thought she couldn't paint because she was so busy with the store all the time.

But maybe she just hadn't found the right inspiration.

Until now.

"You know why I asked you out here?" Seth's voice interrupted her musings.

"You wanted to show off your private cove to as many unsuspecting maidens as you could get your hands on?" She glanced over at him, wondering if the "talking only" rule could be lifted yet. She could definitely envision a ravishing scenario on this rock.

He leaned closer. "I wanted to give some credence to the legend I dreamed up yesterday."

Her pulse knocked hard at her throat, her limbs. Her mind struggled to recall if there were any ravishings detailed in the myth he'd penned.

All she could recall was the part where the couple fell in love.

Swallowing hard, she met his dark gaze. "Which part exactly, were you hoping to fulfill?"

"The part where he digs in his pirate booty," he reached inside his wet shorts pocket. "And pulls out a bauble to tell the rest of the world, hands off, she's with me." He tugged a damp velvet box from his pocket and opened it with all the flourish of a treasure chest.

"Marry me, Mia."

Inside nestled one fat diamond and two perfect rubies on either side of it. All set in a single gold band.

Speechless, Mia gaped at the box.

Seth frowned. "I've done it wrong, haven't I?"

"It's just that there was nothing about baubles or marriage in that legend." She would have definitely remembered that part. Besides, something more essential was missing from his version of the pirate myth, something she knew darn well had been there.

"I fell in love with my captive, Mia, and I want to be with you forever." He cradled her face and set the box on the rock between them. "I can't believe I forgot the most important part."

The old Mia, the one who liked to deny the abandonment issues she'd practically been born with, almost didn't want to believe him. "You've lived with women for years and not fallen in love with them. How can you know you love me let alone that you want to be with me forever?"

Would he still want her after she quizzed him about this? Hope and fear wrestled inside her.

"It took me years to figure out what I *didn't* want, but it only took me one kidnapping to know what I do want." He curled one strand of her straight, damp hair around his finger, his eyes locked on hers. The soft colors of dusk imbued him with a mythical light, making his legendary love feel very real.

"Nobody's messing around with my business," Mia warned. "I've worked hard to stand up to my grandparents and my mother and I'm not about to get steamrolled by any man, no matter how smart his business decisions are."

"You'll have to drag an answer out of me," he promised, sidling closer and nudging the ring on to her lap.

"And that's another thing. If I'm going to allow myself to love you, it's because I'm in love with *you*, not how much you can help me."

The corners of his mouth kicked up into a definite grin. "Admit it, Mia."

"What?"

"You're crazy about me."

"You bet that gorgeous bauble I am." She wrapped both arms around his neck. "I think I fell in love with you the night of the blue paint, but I've been too confused ever since then to know what to do about it."

His mouth found hers, teased and delighted hers with a few sweeps of his tongue, a gentle suckle of her lower lip.

"I know exactly what we can do about it." He leaned back slightly and handed her the ring box. "Hold onto this tight so we don't lose it."

He scooped her off the rock and carried her toward the water.

"I don't think a swim is going to cool me off this time," she protested, holding her rubies with both hands.

Her pirate waded into the water with her anyway. "We're not swimming. And we're definitely done talking."

Oh. Talking time was over.

Her skin flushed at the thought of what exactly *that* meant.

The ravishing had only just begun.

Epilogue

One Year Later

SETH CHANDLER flipped up his eye patch and leaned against the railing of the *Jose Gaspar* to study the throng of festivalgoers lining the fast-approaching shore. He couldn't think of anywhere he'd rather be today. Not while his bride of three months waited in the crowd for him.

He scanned the masses for a red hibiscus, but all he found were string bikinis.

Brock and Noelle stood out among the mob thanks to Brock's bizarre clothing choice. Somehow his uncle had taken a shine to wearing T-shirts advertising his wife's moped shop. Today's shirt was neon orange emblazoned with a sleek black motorbike. No doubt Noelle had ordered the shirts in the most outrageous colors available just to tease Brock, but patient fisherman types didn't ruffle easily. Seth had to admit, Brock wore the "Ride Me…to Bikes 'n Bites" with considerable style.

As the boat docked and the other pirates prepared to leap into the crowd, Seth grew impatient to see that familiar red flower. To see Mia's seductive smile meant just for him.

He gripped the rope in his hands, waiting until the last possible second to jump. He spotted Mia's grandparents wearing matching "Proud To Be a Snowbird" shirts. Ever since Mia had talked them into semiretirement they'd rediscovered their love of travel and spent half the year indulging their adventurous sides.

But where was Mia?

Unable to wait any longer, Seth sailed out over the crowd, landing in the midst of three string bikinis and a grandma with great legs that would have been just his type at last year's Gasparilla.

No more. Only one woman would ever be his type again. Before he could search every inch of the crowd to find her, however, Mia practically fell into his lap.

All at once, she was plastered against him, a slender but curvy-in-all-the-right-places body molded to his and reminded him just how much he loved being married.

Her voice purred low against his ear. "Do we have a date today, sailor, or am I going to have to start screaming to get a little attention?"

He scooped her off her feet, eager to ditch the eye patch for more intimate games. "You have my complete attention, Carmen."

She walked her fingers up his chest, seeming utterly at ease with being carried through the crowd and not caring who might be looking their way.

"I wouldn't want you to go all noble on me again this year," she warned him, waggling her fingers in greeting at a passing television camera.

"Noble? It's all I can do not to sprint right now I want you so bad. I don't think you're going to have to worry about that." He arrived at his boat just in time to prove his point and stepped aboard.

He couldn't help but notice Jesse's boat was parked in the slip next to his, a sure sign his brother was tearing up the festival with a certain lady pirate.

"So this time around you're going to notice if I start pulling off my clothes?" Mia unfastened a button on her blouse, giving him a glimpse of a bright yellow bathing suit underneath the black silk.

Seth couldn't move down the stairs fast enough. This woman kept him in the best shape of his life. She was even proving to have a pretty mean hook shot in their recreational basketball games, but Seth still preferred the more sensual forms of exercise.

"This year, I'm going to beg you not to stop," Seth promised as he fell with her onto the white linen comforter Mia had bought for the bed in the main cabin.

With her love of sensuality and her eye for beauty, Mia created rich settings for their whole lives. She applied her artistic talent to everything from the half-naked mural of them adorning one wall to the white comforter they rolled around on—to the red satin sheets that lay beneath.

"Do tell, Don Jose." Mia unfastened the halter-top of her swimsuit and let it fall away from her breasts. "Begging sounds a bit kinky."

Seth spied the outline of her nipples beneath the silk of her blouse. He manipulated the buttons in record time and had her naked and sighing before she could remember her taunt.

How could he be this hungry for her when they'd just woke up together—and tested the strength of the bathroom sink—three hours ago?

"Begging *does* sound kinky." Seth took up the game, only too happy to tease Mia into delirium. His wife had been a sensual creature to start with, but their year together had taught them both how to perfect one another's pleasure, how to maximize every kiss and caress to heighten sensation.

He smiled as her body began to arch under the gentle massage of his fingertip between her thighs. "In fact, you're welcome to give it a try."

"Please," she moaned, stilling his hand with her own. "I want you." She opened her eyes to stare up at him, her cheeks flushed, her lips full and soft. "All of you."

They climbed between the scarlet sheets with Seth losing the rest of his clothes on the way. He slid inside her without the hindrance of a condom or any other protective device. She wanted a baby one day, and Seth had taken on the mission with all the determination and drive that had brought him to the top of his field.

As he buried himself deep inside her, he thought for the thousandth time that there were so many things he loved about being married. The fact that he and Mia were so happy ranked at the top of the list. But number two wasn't too far behind...

Nowadays, instead of Mia having orgasms from the slow rocking of the boat, Seth gave Mia orgasms that set the whole boat rocking. Along with any other watercraft in the vicinity.

And as Mia scratched at his back and whispered exactly what she would do for him later tonight, Seth took great pride in providing her with one right about… Now.

The Trueblood, Texas
tradition continues in...

 HARLEQUIN® *Blaze*™

TRULY, MADLY, DEEPLY
by Vicki Lewis Thompson
August 2002

Ten years ago, Dustin Ramsey and Erica Mann shared their first
sexual experience. It was a disaster. Now Dustin's determined to
find—and seduce—Erica again, to prove to her, and himself, that
he can do better. Much, *much* better. Only, little does he guess
that Erica's got the same agenda....

Don't miss Blaze's next two sizzling Trueblood tales:

EVERY MOVE YOU MAKE by Tori Carrington
September 2002
&
LOVE ON THE ROCKS by Debbi Rawlins
October 2002

Available wherever Harlequin books are sold.

TRUEBLOOD, TEXAS

HARLEQUIN®
Makes any time special®

More fabulous reading from
the Queen of Sizzle!

LORI
FOSTER

with

Forever and Always

Back by popular demand are the scintillating stories of
Gabe and Jordan Buckhorn. They're gorgeous, sexy
and single…at least for now!

Available wherever books are sold—September 2002.

And look for Lori's *brand-new* single title,
CASEY in early 2003

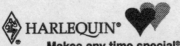

"I don't trust either of us near that bed, Mia."

Seth placed his hand on Mia's knee, the heat of his palm penetrating her skin. "But I have something else in mind."

She wondered if it was possible to melt at a man's touch. If so, she stood a very good chance of pooling at Seth's feet any moment, because his hand on her knee made her whole body turn warm and liquid. He walked his fingers up the outside of her thigh until his hand landed on her hip. Then he scooted her close to him and angled his lips over hers.

The man planned to drug her with his aphrodisiac kisses and then coax her into orgasmic heaven. All of which sounded delightful, except...

"That's not fair to you." She broke off their kiss, much to her lips' regret.

"It's perfectly fair," he whispered, leaning forward to reclaim her mouth.

Mia needed to take action before he had her talked into becoming erotically dependent on him. She slid her fingers down his chest to the waistband of his shorts, smoothing her hand over the ridge there.

"I bet I send you into orbit without ever hitting the sheets."

Dear Reader,

As much as I love sizzling contemporary romance, there is also a place in my heart for a hot historical, too. Imagine my pleasure when I discovered a way to rope these two loves together in the opening pages of *Wild and Willing*. Tampa, Florida's Gasparilla festival allowed me to write a modern-day pirate sailing into harbor, ready to carry off the damsel of his choice.

Of course, this being a Blaze novel, the heroine had to be every bit as bold and brash as her pirate hero. In steps Mia Quentin, modern maiden on a mission! She's not only ready and willing to indulge in a sexy kidnapping scenario with Seth Chandler, she's out to make sure he can't possibly choose anyone but her for potential ravishing.

If you enjoy Seth and Mia's steamy Florida adventures, don't miss my 2003 Blaze title, *Wild and Wicked,* which revisits Gasparilla and all the fun that ensues. Seth's brother Jesse has his own story to tell—a tale that involves a lusty lady pirate determined to make Jesse see the sensual potential in their friendship! Visit me at www.JoanneRock.com to learn more about my future releases or to let me know what you think of my books. I'd love to hear from you!

Happy reading,

Joanne Rock

P.S.—Don't forget to check out www.tryblaze.com!

Books by Joanne Rock

HARLEQUIN BLAZE
26—SILK, LACE & VIDEOTAPE
48—IN HOT PURSUIT

HARLEQUIN TEMPTATION
863—LEARNING CURVES